An English Murder

CYRIL HARE

FABER & FABER

This edition first published in 2017
by Faber & Faber Ltd
Bloomsbury House
74–77 Great Russell Street
London WC1B 3DA
This edition first published in the USA in 2017

Typeset by Faber & Faber Ltd
Printed and bound by CPI Group (UK) Ltd, Croydon, CRO 4YY

A CIP record for this book is available from the British Library

ISBN 978-0-571-33901-3

FSC
www.fsc.org
MIX
Paper from
responsible sources
FSC® C020471

2 4 6 8 10 9 7 5 3 1

Cyril Hare was the pseudonym for the distinguished lawyer Alfred Alexander Gordon Clark. He was born in Surrey, in 1900, and was educated at Rugby and Oxford. A member of the Inner Temple, he was called to the Bar in 1924 and joined the chambers of Roland Oliver, who handled many of the great crime cases of the 1920s. He practised as a barrister until the Second World War, after which he served in various legal and judicial capacities including a time as a county court judge in Surrey.

Hare's crime novels, many of which draw on his legal experience, have been praised by Elizabeth Bowen and P. D. James among others. He died in 1958 – at the peak of his career as a judge, and at the height of his powers as a master of the whodunit.

I

The Butler and the Professor

Warbeck Hall is reputed to be the oldest inhabited house in Markshire. The muniment room in the north-eastern angle is probably its oldest part; it is certainly the coldest. Dr Wenceslaus Bottwink, PhD, of Heidelberg, Hon. DLitt of Oxford, sometime Professor of Modern History in the University of Prague, corresponding member of half a dozen learned societies from Leyden to Chicago, felt the cold sink into his bones as he sat bowed over the pages of a pile of faded manuscripts, pausing now and then in his reading to transcribe passages from them in his angular foreign script. He was accustomed to cold. It had been cold in his student's lodgings in Heidelberg, colder yet in Prague in the winter of 1917, coldest of all in the concentration camps of the Third Reich. He was conscious of it, but so long as he could keep his fingers from growing too stiff to hold a pen, he did not allow it to affect his concentration. It was no more than a tiresome background to his work. The real obstacle that was worrying him at the moment was the atrocious handwriting in which the third Viscount Warbeck had annotated the confidential letters written to him by Lord Bute during the first three years of the reign of George III. Those marginalia! Those crabbed, truncated interlineations! Dr Bottwink had begun to feel a personal grievance against this eighteenth-century patrician. That a man who had been the recipient of such important information, the guardian of secrets of state of such inestimable value to succeeding generations, should have had sufficient sense of his duty to posterity to preserve them intact, and then should choose to record the most precious confidences of all in illegible scribbles – it was unbearable! It was entirely due to him that the investigation of the Warbeck papers had taken more than twice the time that had been set aside for it. And time was so precious to an ageing scholar whose health was not what it had been! It would be *his* fault if the work that was to lay bare the development of the English constitution between 1750 and 1784 remained incomplete at its author's death. Dr Bottwink stared in angry bewilderment at the hieroglyphics before him and across two centuries muttered maledictions on Lord Warbeck and his ill-mended quill pen.

There was a discreet knock at the door, and, without waiting for an answer, a manservant came into the room. He was a stout, elderly man, with the non-committal expression common to butlers in good houses.

'I have brought you your tea, sir,' he said, depositing a tray on the table in the middle of the room.

'Thank you, Briggs,' said Dr Bottwink. 'That is very kind of you. You really should not take the trouble.'

'It is no trouble, sir. I generally have a cup myself about this time, and this is only one flight of stairs up from the pantry.'

Dr Bottwink nodded gravely. He was sufficiently familiar with English customs to know that even today a butler does not normally give his reasons for serving tea to a guest in the house. It was precisely because he was not quite on the footing of a guest that Briggs found it necessary to explain why it was no trouble to climb a flight of stairs. Dr Bottwink savoured the delicate social distinction with a certain wry pleasure.

'None the less, it is kind of you, Briggs,' he insisted, in his careful English. 'Even though we are such close neighbours. Between us, we are the only inhabitants of the original building of Warbeck Hall.'

'Quite so, sir. This part of the house was actually built by Perkin Warbeck himself in the year—'

'Ah, no, Briggs!' Dr Bottwink paused in the act of pouring himself a cup of tea to correct him. 'You may say that sort of thing to visitors and tourists, but you must not say it to *me*. In fact, Perkin Warbeck is a myth – not historically speaking a myth, I mean, but in regard to Lord Warbeck's family. There is no connection at all. This branch of the Warbecks has a quite different origin and a much more respectable one, I assure you. It is all in the documents up there.' He nodded towards an oak press against the wall behind him.

'Well, sir,' replied Briggs suavely, 'that is what we say in Markshire, at any rate.'

Whatever retort Dr Bottwink was about to make, he thought better of it. Instead, he murmured quietly to himself, 'What we say in Markshire today ...' and gulped his tea. Aloud he said, 'This tea is very comforting, Briggs. It warms the cockles.' He glanced a little proudly at the butler to see if his command of English idiom was appreciated.

Briggs permitted himself the ghost of a smile.

'Just so, sir,' he said. 'It is very cold. There seems to be snow in the air. To judge from the forecast, we may expect a white Christmas.'

'Christmas!' Dr Bottwink put down his cup. 'Is it as late in the year as that? One loses all account of time in a place like this. Are we really near to Christmas?'

'The day after tomorrow, sir.'

'I had no idea. I have been so much longer on this job than I intended. I have trespassed on Lord Warbeck's hospitality long enough as it is. Perhaps it will be inconvenient for him to keep me here at such a time. I should ask him.'

'I took the liberty, sir, of raising the subject with his lordship just now when I brought him his tea, and he expressed the desire that if it met with your convenience you should remain as his guest over the festive season.'

'That is very kind of him. I shall take the opportunity of thanking him personally, if he is able to see me. How is he today, by the way?'

'His lordship is better, thank you, sir. He is up, but not yet down.'

'Up, but not yet down,' repeated Dr Bottwink thoughtfully. 'Up, but not down! English is a beautifully expressive language!'

'Quite, sir.'

'By the way, Briggs, you spoke just now of the festive season. I imagine that in present circumstances the festivities will be of a purely notional character?'

'I beg your pardon, sir?'

'I mean, there will in fact be no junketings, no – no—' He snapped his fingers impatiently as the phrase eluded him. '– No high jinks?'

'I am unable to say, sir, precisely what form the celebrations will take; but I think it may be assumed that Christmas will be quiet. His lordship has only invited a few members of his family.'

'Oh! There are to be guests, then? Who, for example?'

'Sir Julius arrives this evening, sir, and tomorrow—'

'Sir Julius?'

'Sir Julius Warbeck, sir.'

'But he is Chancellor of the Exchequer in the present government, is he not?'

'Precisely, sir.'

'I thought, from my conversations with him, that Lord Warbeck's political views were of a very different character.'

'His politics, sir? Sir Julius is coming here, I understand, simply in his capacity as Lord Warbeck's first cousin.'

Dr Bottwink sighed.

'After all these years,' he said, 'I sometimes feel that I shall never understand England. Never.'

'Will you be requiring me any further, sir?'

'I apologise, Briggs. My vulgar continental curiosity is keeping you from your work.'

'Not at all, sir.'

'Then if you can bear to remain in this ice-house a moment longer, I should be glad if you would tell me something else which is of some importance to me. How exactly do I stand in the house during these Christmas festivities?'

'Sir?'

'It would be as well that I should efface myself, would

it not? Lord Warbeck has been good enough to treat me as his guest while I have been here, but naturally I should not expect to be on quite the same footing as members of his family – particularly while his lordship is up and not down. It is rather a delicate situation, eh, Briggs?'

The butler coughed.

'Were you referring to meals, sir?' he asked.

'Well, yes, meals are the crucial point, I suppose. I can occupy myself very well up here at other times. What is your advice?'

'I ventured to mention the problem to his lordship just now. The difficulty, as you will appreciate, sir, is one of staff.'

'I confess I had not altogether appreciated that difficulty.'

'In the old days, sir,' Briggs went on reminiscently, 'there would have been no trouble. There would have been four in the kitchen and two footmen under me, and of course the servants the visiting ladies and gentlemen brought would have been available to assist. But as things are, with me being single-handed, as I told his lordship, I really could not undertake to serve meals separate. One service in the dining-room and one in the servants' hall is as much as I can manage – with a tray upstairs for his lordship, of course. So if you don't mind, sir—'

'I quite understand, Briggs. I shall be honoured to have my meals with you while the guests are here.'

'Oh, no, sir! I did not mean that at all. I wouldn't have dreamt of even suggesting such a thing to his lordship.'

Dr Bottwink realised that once more, despite his best endeavours, he had been guilty of a social *faux pas*. 'Well,' he said resignedly, 'I am in your hands, Briggs. Then I am to take my meals with the family party?'

'If you don't mind, sir.'

'Mind? How should I? It is to be hoped that they will not mind. I shall be delighted to meet Sir Julius, at any rate. He can enlighten me on some points of constitutional practice which I still find rather obscure. Perhaps you can tell me who else I am to meet?'

'There are just two ladies, sir, Lady Camilla Prendergast and Mrs Carstairs.'

'Lady Prendergast is a member of the family also?'

'Not Lady Prendergast, sir – Lady Camilla Prendergast. A courtesy title. She is addressed as Lady Camilla, being an earl's daughter. She is a niece of her late ladyship's first husband. We count her as a member of the family. Mrs Carstairs is not related, but her father was rector of this parish for many years and she was brought up in the house, so to speak. That is all the party – except for Mr Robert, of course.'

'Mr Robert Warbeck, the son of the house – he is to be here for Christmas?'

'Naturally, sir.'

'Yes.' Dr Bottwink was speaking to himself. 'I suppose it is natural. Curious that I should not have thought of him.' He turned to the butler. 'Briggs, I suppose it would be impossible for me to have my meals in the servants' hall after all?'

'Sir?'

'I don't think I shall greatly enjoy sitting down at table with Mr Robert Warbeck.'

'*Sir?*'

'Oh, now I have shocked you, Briggs, and I should not have done that. But you know who Mr Robert is?'

'Of course I do, sir. His lordship's son and heir.'

'I am not thinking of him in that capacity. Do you not know that he is the president of this affair that calls itself the League of Liberty and Justice?'

'I understand that to be the fact, sir.'

'The League of Liberty and Justice, Briggs,' said Dr Bottwink very clearly and deliberately, 'is a Fascist organisation.'

'Is that so, sir?'

'You are not interested, Briggs?'

'I have never been greatly interested in politics, sir.'

'Oh, Briggs, Briggs,' said the historian, shaking his head in regretful admiration, 'if you only knew how fortunate you were to be able to say just that!'

II

The Guests

Sir Julius Warbeck allowed the rug to be adjusted over his knees, exchanged a few last words with his secretary, and leaned back wearily against the cushions as the car drove away from Downing Street. On the seat beside him was an official bag, containing the latest report on the vital negotiations then being conducted in Washington on behalf of the Treasury with the government of the United States. It was there to occupy him during the two hours' drive to Warbeck, so that not a moment of the Chancellor's precious official time should be wasted; but the car had threaded the maze of central London and began to cruise smoothly along the arterial road before Sir Julius made a move towards it.

He drew the bag on to his knees, unlocked it and began to study the closely typed sheets. It was an admirably written report, he reflected, as one might expect from Carstairs. He felt a little pride as he remembered that Carstairs had been his discovery in the first place. There could have been few who foresaw ten years ago the position that that young man was likely to attain, and Sir Julius, who was not usually slow to give himself credit for his own achievements, gave himself full credit for having been one of them.

Dun-coloured clouds, threatening snow, obscured the wintry sky, and the figures began to dance before the

Chancellor's tired eyes. He was glad to take the excuse to return the report half-read to the bag, and to lean back again in his seat. Carstairs! The name recurred to him with a hint of irritation. Yes, undoubtedly that fellow had come a long way and was going further yet. More than one informed writer had spoken of him as the next Chancellor of the Exchequer, and Sir Julius, with the realism of an experienced politician, admitted to himself that nobody could last for ever and that he should be thankful that there should be such capable shoulders waiting to take up the burden, when the time came for him to lay it down. (Not that that time was likely to come soon, whatever some people, Carstairs included, might be inclined to think!) But he had to admit to himself that in his heart of hearts he did not like his brilliant young colleague. There was something about the man, for all his undoubted charm and talent, that was not quite – the dreadful words *well bred* flickered in his mind. He exorcised them with a shudder. This would never do! Alan Carstairs was an excellent fellow. It was not his fault – it was very much to his credit – that he had risen in the world with so few initial advantages. Remembering his own assured background, he ran over in his mind the pattern of Carstairs' career. Elementary school, scholarships, the London School of Economics, a fortunate marriage – yes, a very fortunate marriage, Sir Julius reflected. Without the encouragement of that active, ambitious woman, would he have ever got anywhere, for all his brains? Mrs Carstairs was to be at Warbeck, his cousin had told him. 'I must remember to say something civil to her about her husband,' he said to himself. Somehow he always found it difficult to be civil to Mrs Carstairs. She had a way of belittling all politicians except her beloved Alan. And Sir Julius did not relish being belittled.

He sat for a time staring absently in front of him. Beyond the glass partition he could see the rigid backs of the two silent men sitting in front. Their stiffness and impersonality, even towards each other, affronted him. Why should officialdom always tend to turn men into automatons? Sir Julius liked to think of himself as a genial, friendly type of man, conscious – as was only proper – of his own position and what was due to it, but within proper limits human and approachable. But try as he would, he had never succeeded in getting on proper terms with these two. There must be something wrong with them. Holly, the driver, was not so bad. His people lived near Markhampton, and Sir Julius had been at some pains to arrange that he should take the car on to his home over Christmas, calling at Warbeck Hall for the return journey after the holiday. He had at least shown some gratitude for the gesture, though not as much as might have been expected. But the other man – Rogers – the detective assigned to him by the Special Branch of Scotland Yard – what could one make of him? Sometimes he wondered whether Rogers was human at all. For the last three months the man had been his constant shadow, and he was no nearer to knowing him than he had been at the beginning. The fellow was quiet, civil, answered when spoken to, and that was all that there was to it. No doubt he should consider himself lucky that Rogers possessed no actively disagreeable quality – unlike the dreadful man who had preceded him and sniffed continually – but he remained dissatisfied. It was disheartening to be so much in the company of a man on whom one could make no impression. That, if he had but known it, was the root of the whole trouble. Sir Julius, vain gregarious soul that he was, had made his career by impressing other people. It was a cruel fate that had given him for guardian a man whom the warm rays of his personality impressed no more than if they had been the cold beams of the moon.

By now a few flakes of snow had begun to strike against the windscreen and the wiper was clicking back and forth with the persistence of a metronome. The car had left the main road and was following a route that, in spite of the gathering darkness, was more and more familiar to the eyes of the elderly man sitting inside. As the miles passed, it seemed to become almost an extension of his own personality in the way that only places known and loved from childhood can. For it was no longer a road leading from London into Markshire; it was the way to Warbeck. And as he travelled, something very strange occurred inside the Right Honourable Sir Julius Warbeck, MP, Chancellor of the Exchequer in the most advanced socialist government of Western Europe. He was fifteen years old, up from Eton to spend the Christmas holidays with his uncle; and as one remembered landmark succeeded another, he felt again that curious blend of pride at belonging to one of the oldest families in England and envy for his cousin, the heir to all the splendours of that lovely place. When the car slowed down to negotiate the hump-backed bridge over the stream that separated Warbeck village from the demesne, he even found himself, forty years after, reviling the fate that had made his father a younger son and deprived him of the position he would have filled with such dignity and grace.

The jolting of the car on the ill-kept drive effectually broke the spell. Sir Julius abruptly found himself back in mid-twentieth century, in a world where the owners of historic mansions were pitiable anachronisms, helplessly awaiting the hour when the advancing tread of social justice would force them from the privileged positions they had too long usurped. (The phrases of his last election address came back to him with triumphant satisfaction. The envious schoolboy of forty years ago was avenged!) Not that he felt any ill will towards his cousin. He appreciated the gesture he had made in inviting the representative of the new order to the family home for the last time – and he had shown his appreciation by accepting. But quite certainly it was for the last time. Lord Warbeck was not long for this world. He had made that clear enough in his letter of invitation. After him there would be no more Warbecks of Warbeck Hall. The next Budget would see to that. It was just as well. The old order would disappear with a decent and dignified representative at least. As for young Robert— At the very thought of Robert Warbeck and all that he stood for, the Chancellor's blood boiled in his veins, so that it was an unreasonably flushed and angry man that alighted from his car at the end of the journey.

'What train are you taking tomorrow, Camilla?' the Countess of Simnel asked her daughter.

'The two o'clock. I'm lunching with the Carstairs woman first and we'll be travelling down together.'

'I see. Won't you find that rather dull?'

Lady Camilla laughed.

'I expect I shall,' she said. 'But I haven't any choice. That's the train Uncle Tom has arranged to have met, and I can't afford to pay for a taxi out from the station for myself, so that's the train I have to take. Anyhow, travelling with her saves one the trouble of making conversation. One needn't listen to her, either. So long as one looks intelligent, she'll go on talking all day about her marvellous Alan without expecting one to answer.'

'Mrs Carstairs,' observed Lady Simnel succinctly, 'is a bore. At the same time, there is something admirable in her devotion to her husband. A woman is lucky who has found a purpose in life, as she has done.'

Lady Camilla said nothing, but the expression on her handsome, intelligent face showed that she understood more in the words than their surface meaning.

'It will be chilly at Warbeck at this time of year,' her mother went on. 'I hope you are taking plenty of warm things.'

'I'm taking everything I've got. And what's more, I intend to wear it all. All at once. I shall positively bulge with clothes. I know what Warbeck can be in a cold snap.'

'Don't you think you would be more comfortable spending Christmas quietly with me in London?'

Lady Camilla looked round the small, well-furnished drawing-room of her mother's flat and smiled.

'Much more comfortable, Mother dear,' she agreed.

'You really think it is worth your while to go?'

'But of course I've got to go, Mother. Uncle Tom particularly asked me. And as this may be my last chance of seeing the old dear——'

Lady Simnel sniffed. Whether it was because of some

particularly forbidding quality in the sniff, or because her words did not sound very convincing even to herself, Camilla left the sentence hanging in mid-air.

'Robert will be there, I suppose?' Lady Simnel asked abruptly.

'Robert? Oh yes, I suppose so. Sure to be.'

'How long is it since you last saw him, Camilla?'

'I don't know exactly. Quite a time. He – he's been very busy lately.'

'Very busy,' said Lady Simnel dryly. 'If you can call this imbecile League of Liberty and whatever-it-is a business. Too busy to have any time to spare for his old friends, at any rate.'

'Robert,' said Camilla, rather breathlessly, 'is a very brave man. He proved that in the war. And what is more, he is a patriot. One may not agree with all his views, but that's no reason for abusing him.'

'Well,' her mother replied calmly, 'you are twenty-five, and old enough to know your own mind. Quite apart from his politics, I don't think that Robert is any great catch, myself. It isn't as though he would ever be able to afford to live at Warbeck. But that's your affair. I don't believe in interfering in matters of this kind. As for abusing him, all I did was to point out that he has been avoiding you for some time past.'

'Look here, Mother!' Lady Camilla turned abruptly in her chair to look her mother in the face. 'You think I'm running after Robert, don't you?'

'Well, my dear, I don't know what the modern expression is for that sort of thing, but that's what it would have been called in my day.'

'Then you're quite right – I am. And when I get to Warbeck I mean to have it out with him one way or the other. I can't go on like this – I can't. If he doesn't want me, let him just say so, and not try to back out of things by keeping out of the way. And why the hell should he *not* want me, I should like to know?'

Lady Camilla stood up, a magnificent figure of a young woman. Her mother looked at her with disillusioned, appraising eyes.

'It might be because he wanted someone else,' she observed. 'But you had better go to Warbeck and find out, as you say – one way or the other.'

Mrs Carstairs was speaking to Washington on the transatlantic telephone. Her voice poured out into the mouthpiece in hurried gusts of speech, with only the briefest intervals for a reply. It was as if she was determined to get the greatest possible value in words for her three-minute call.

'Marvellous to hear your voice, darling,' she was saying. 'You're not feeling too tired after all your work? . . . And you're sure you're getting proper food? . . . Oh, of course, dear, I *know* you are, but you have to be so careful with your digestion . . . You will promise me you won't overdo it, won't you? . . . You know, I ought really to be there to look after you . . . Yes, dear, I know, and after all I am doing my little bit to hold the fort while you are away. I wrote and told you I was going to Warbeck for Christmas, didn't I? . . . Oh, yes, the Chancellor will be there, silly pompous old man . . . Well, perhaps I shouldn't, but you know he *is*. It makes me mad to think of him standing in your way, when everybody knows . . . No, dear, of course I won't. I shall be very polite to him. I think he realises now just how much he owes to you . . . Darling, you're much too modest. If you only knew how proud I feel of you. I saw the PM on Tuesday, and the things he said about you made me so happy . . . Darling, that was sweet of you. Of course I'd do anything in the world to help you, but it's little enough a poor, weak woman can do . . . Yes, I go down to Warbeck tomorrow. It will be nice to be there again. I only wish you could be there with me . . . Alan, dear, don't be so *absurd*! Of course you wouldn't be out of place anywhere! Don't you realise that you are a great man now? Why, I shall simply be basking in your reflected glory . . . Oh, no, it isn't a house-party – simply a little family gathering . . . Yes, Robert will be there, I'm afraid . . . I know, darling, *horrid*, but it can't be helped. It's a pity, he used to be such a nice boy . . . But, darling, you don't really think this League of his can be *dangerous*, do you? . . . No, no, of course one can't discuss it over the telephone, but a nod's as good as a wink, and I promise I'll be very careful . . . Yes, darling, you can trust me, you know, to do everything I can. I always have, haven't I? . . . Oh, Alan, dearest, if you only knew how proud I feel. The *Daily Trumpet* had a marvellous article all about you yesterday, on the leader page. It made me laugh! When one thinks how the *Trumpet* used to—' And so on, and on, and on.

In a gaunt room on the upper floor of a disused warehouse in South London, Robert Warbeck was concluding a monthly conference of section leaders of the League of Liberty and Justice. He was a tall, good-looking young man with red-brown hair and the fixed look of a fanatic in his rather prominent grey eyes. The dozen or so men he had been addressing for the last half-hour were a mixed collection of all types and classes. None were more than thirty-five years of age. The common factor that united them, apart from the complete absorption with which they hung upon their leader's words, was their dress. In common with him, each wore a pair of grey flannel trousers and a purple pullover, on the left breast of which was embroidered a white dagger.

'That will be all for this evening, gentlemen. You will be notified in due course of the date of the next conference. You are dismissed.'

Each man rose from his chair, stood for a moment at attention and executed a somewhat complicated salute with the left hand which Robert Warbeck gravely returned. There then followed a moment of anticlimax. Retiring to the back of the room, the men stripped off their pullovers, handed them to one of their number and trooped out in their shirtsleeves, to resume downstairs the coats and waistcoats of civil life.

Warbeck was left alone with the man who had received the garments. He watched in silence while they were ceremoniously folded up and put away in a large cupboard which ran the length of the room. Then he stretched himself wearily, removed his own and handed it to his lieutenant, to be put away in a special locked compartment of its own.

'The time is coming,' he said, 'when we shall wear the uniform in public. But that time is not yet.'

'Yes, chief.' The reply was respectful, but a shade perfunctory, as from a man who had heard the same remark many times before. 'The key of your cupboard, chief.'

'Thank you.'

'You look tired, chief.'

'I shall be glad of a few days' rest,' Warbeck admitted, as though ashamed to confess to a human weakness.

'You leave town tomorrow, chief?'

'Yes. I shall look in at the Fulham branch on my way out of London. Those fellows want to learn the meaning of discipline.'

'You'll teach them, chief.'

'I shall be back at the beginning of next week. We can make arrangements for the North London rally then. Meanwhile you know where you can get in touch with me if necessary.'

'Yes, chief. I hope you have an enjoyable Christmas.'

Warbeck said nothing for a moment. He was knotting his tie and looking reflectively in the glass as he did so.

'Thank you,' he said at last. 'I shall have the enjoyment of doing my duty, at least. One owes something to one's family.'

'I'm afraid you may find your company rather trying, chief,' his attendant ventured.

Warbeck swung round upon him.

'What do you mean?' he asked fiercely.

'Well, chief,' the man stuttered, 'I – I only meant – I was referring to Sir Julius, chief.'

'Julius? What the hell has he got to do with it?'

'But I understood he was spending Christmas at Warbeck Hall, chief. Isn't that correct?'

'It's the first I've heard of it.'

'There was a paragraph in this morning's *Times*, chief. I thought you must know about it.'

'Good God! My father must be—' He checked himself in time. He had almost forgotten the golden rule, never to discuss his personal affairs with subordinates. 'Well, thanks for telling me, Sikes,' he went on, as he put on his coat. 'I had missed the notice in *The Times*. I don't usually read the snobs' page, anyway. Forewarned is forearmed. I shan't be sorry to have the chance of giving that windbag a piece of my mind. Perhaps he won't have such an enjoyable Christmas. Good night!'

'Good night, chief.'

He walked out into the drab street, where the thinly falling snow was fast turning into grey slush.

III

Father and Son

The snow did not start to fall in earnest until after darkness had set in, but once begun it continued with ever-increasing density until well after daybreak. Lord Warbeck, waking from the light sleep of an invalid, saw from his window his lawns and garden with the parkland beyond and the Markshire Downs in the far distance uniformly white, the fine details of the landscape gone, the outlines smoothed and thickened by the covering of snow. It would all have looked exactly the same, he reflected, to anyone lying in that bed on such a morning at any time since Capability Brown remodelled the plantations in the park, nearly two hundred years before. All trace of the neglect and disrepair of recent times had vanished. The drive again ran smooth and straight between its avenue of pollarded limes. The bowling-green for once displayed a surface as flat and true as it had done when it had been the whole duty of an able-bodied man to keep it in order. It was all an illusion, of course. Two days of thaw would suffice to reveal the hummocks and holes and weeds of reality – to reveal, also, he thought grimly, half a dozen burst pipes at different points in the cumbersome old house which he would somehow have to find the money to repair. No matter. For a prematurely aged, sick man, it was pleasant to indulge in the illusion while it lasted – especially as it might be for the last time.

When Briggs brought him his breakfast tray, he said, 'I shall get up after lunch, Briggs.'

'Very good, my lord.'

'I shall want you to help me down to the library then. I shall have tea there with my guests.'

'Dr Curtis said, my lord—'

'Dr Curtis won't come out here in this weather. He's got a weak chest, like his father. Never could stand a cold snap. He needn't know anything about it.'

'No, my lord.'

'How is Sir Julius this morning?'

'Sir Julius appears to be in excellent health, my lord. He breakfasted early – almost as early as Dr Bottwink, in fact – and retired to work in his room. He passed some observation on going to put another sixpence on the income-tax, but I gathered that his intention was to be jocose.'

'Let us hope so, Briggs. It sounds a grim kind of joke to me, but there's no accounting for tastes. Thank goodness, there doesn't seem to be much chance of my living to next Budget day, anyhow.'

'Quite, my lord. That is – I'm sure I beg your lordship's pardon – we all hope—'

'Say no more about it, Briggs. It was tactless of me to refer to the subject.'

'Not at all, my lord, I'm sure.'

Briggs, rather pink about the cheeks, made to retire from the room, but hesitated in the doorway and cleared his throat. Lord Warbeck, who knew the symptoms, looked up from his breakfast.

'What is it, Briggs?' he asked.

'I was not informed, my lord,' the butler said in somewhat reproachful tones, 'that Sir Julius would be bringing a – a person with him.'

'A person? I'm not sure that I— Oh, dear me, yes, of course – the detective. It was stupid of me to have forgotten, but I'm afraid that is the price we have to pay for entertaining Cabinet Ministers. I hope you don't find his presence very disagreeable.'

'No, my lord, I cannot say that exactly. I was a little exercised in my mind as to the matter of his meals. But on consideration I came to the conclusion that the position would be met by arranging for him to feed with the staff.'

'From my limited experience of Scotland Yard, Briggs, I think you did absolutely right,' said Lord Warbeck, gravely. 'I trust that your decision met with the approval of your colleagues?'

'I am bound to say, my lord, that there was at first some little unrest in the kitchen. But it passed over.'

'I am relieved to hear that.'

'The position was greatly eased by the person offering to assist with the washing-up, my lord.'

'Excellent! That appears to solve all your problems, Briggs.'

'There is just this little further matter, my lord. He appears to think he should be given the run of the house.'

'I'm not sure that I altogether follow you.'

'A member of the staff, my lord,' said Briggs severely, 'is normally expected to confine himself to the staff quarters, except for the purposes of his duty. It is difficult nowadays, when we are expected to apply ourselves to duties which are not, strictly speaking, our own, to adhere to this rule in the way that I should wish to see done, but so far as possible, my lord, I like to uphold the traditions of the house.'

'So do I, Briggs, God knows! So do I.'

'Well, my lord, it will be highly unsettling to discipline if this individual, while, socially speaking, a member of the staff, should presume to go wherever he pleases and generally poke his nose into every corner of the house, if I may so express myself, my lord.'

'For the purposes of his duty, Briggs, remember.'

'His duty, my lord?'

'This gentleman's duty, you know, is the personal protection of the Chancellor of the Exchequer.'

'Protection?' Briggs echoed, in an offended tone. 'In this house, my lord?'

'It should certainly be a sinecure in this house, I agree. But I'm afraid, whatever the effect on domestic discipline, you will have to let him carry out his job in his own way.'

'If you say so, my lord.' The butler's tone was loaded with disapproval. 'But it puzzles me to know what he thinks he is protecting Sir Julius from.'

'From anything that is going, I suppose,' said Lord Warbeck, lightly. 'From any terror by night or the arrow that flieth by day.'

Briggs permitted himself to smile. 'And from the pestilence that walketh in darkness, my lord?' he said gently.

'No, Briggs. Even Cabinet Ministers cannot arrange for protection from that.'

Robert Warbeck arrived at the house about four o'clock on Christmas Eve. He was not in the best of tempers. The interview with the Fulham branch of the League of Liberty and Justice had not gone off as well as he had expected, and he had been further delayed by engine trouble while a little way out of London. Then, just as he turned off the main road, the snow had begun to fall again, so that the last few miles of his journey had been increasingly slow and difficult. He was cramped and cold by the time that he brought the car to a standstill at the front door. Briggs came forward at once to take his bag.

'Good afternoon, Mr Robert,' he said. 'I trust you are well?' He spoke respectfully enough, but in a tone which a close observer might have thought somewhat lacking in warmth.

'Yes thanks, Briggs. I'm all right. How is my father?'

'His lordship is better, sir. He is out of bed today and in the library.'

'Good! I'll go up to him directly.'

'Mr Robert, would it be convenient for you before you see his lordship—'

But Robert either did not hear the butler's words or chose to disregard them.

'I'll take the car round to the back now,' he said abruptly. 'Will you put my bag in my room?'

He let in the clutch and the car vanished round the side of the house. Briggs was left at the open front door, the bag in his hand. As he stood there, the snow falling on his bald head, the control which years of domestic service had imposed upon his features momentarily lapsed and a perfectly natural expression appeared upon his face. It was not the expression of a happy man, nor of a man well disposed towards the object of his thoughts.

Robert left the car in the coach-house which served the house for a garage. He spent a little time swathing the bonnet in rugs against the chill air in the vast building, in the further corners of which a few dilapidated carriages still remained from the golden age of horses and prosperity. Then he walked quickly along the range of tenantless loose-boxes, crossed the stable yard and entered the house by a side door. Moving quietly and quickly, almost as if he were anxious to avoid being noticed, he made his way thence to the hall, and, pausing there only long enough to rid himself of his overcoat, went directly into the library.

Lord Warbeck was lying on a sofa drawn up close to the fire. He had been dozing, but started into life at the sound of the opening door. A flush came to his pale cheeks and he sat up as he realised who the newcomer was.

'Robert, dear boy, it's good to see you!' he exclaimed.

'Good to see you, Father. Sorry I'm so late, but I've had a simply poisonous journey here.'

Robert came across the room to the sofa, and there ensued a minute, but perceptible, pause which a foreign observer such as Dr Bottwink, had he been present, would have noticed with interest. In any other European country, a reunion in such circumstances would have been signalised by an embrace. That was obviously out of the question. Robert, naturally, had given up the practice of kissing his father since he first went into long trousers. When they met they shook hands as English people should. But there is something rather absurd about shaking hands with a man who is lying down. Eventually he compromised by placing one hand lightly on his father's shoulder.

'Sit down over there,' said Lord Warbeck gruffly, as though a little ashamed at his son's display of emotion. He indicated a chair on the other side of the fireplace. 'You're looking well.'

'Yes, thanks, I'm very fit,' said Robert. 'And you're look-ing—' He paused, and his voice took on a tinge of anxiety. 'How are you feeling, Father?'

'Much the same as usual,' said Lord Warbeck quietly. 'I am feeling quietly expectant, waiting for the aneurism to blow up, or whatever aneurisms do. It's three months now since young Curtis told me I shouldn't live to see Christ-mas, and now with only a few hours to go I think I should do it. Indeed I'm relying on you to tide me over Boxing Day. Nothing could be more ill-bred in a host than to choose such a moment to expire.'

Robert's face, which had until then expressed nothing but sympathetic interest, took on a look of sullen disap-proval at the word 'host'.

'You've asked Julius here,' he said in a low, level voice.

'Yes. Did I mention it when I wrote last?'

'No. One of my fellows told me. He'd seen it in the paper.'

'Well, the paper is right for once. Julius is here now, and, according to Briggs, is filling in time putting some-thing on the income-tax.'

'I don't think that's very funny.' Robert looked so ab-surdly like a sulky small boy as he said this, glowering over the fire, that his father, torn between affection and irritation, found it difficult to suppress a smile. But he contrived to keep his voice under control as he answered.

'It's not a good joke, I admit, but it appears to have been Julius's. You must blame him for it, not me. In any case, I do not need telling that income-tax is no laughing matter.'

'That's not the point,' Robert persisted.

'No, I gathered that. Your objection is to Julius per-sonally.'

'Of course it is. How could you allow him to come here, Father – *him* of all people?'

'Listen to me, Robert.' Lord Warbeck's voice, though feeble, had in it the authentic note of authority. 'You and I have not always agreed on everything, but I think that in your own way you feel as deeply as I do about the traditions of our family and the traditions of this dear old house. As far back as I can remember, and further than that, Christmas at Warbeck has meant the reunion of our family and our friends. There's not much left of the family now. Yourself excepted, Julius is the only near relation I have alive. And since this looks like being my last Christmas on earth, I should think poorly of myself if I were to break with that tradition now. That is why I thought it proper to offer him hospitality.'

'And can you tell me why he thought proper to accept it?' Robert broke in. 'You talk of tradition, Father. Have you ever tried talking about it to Julius? He's the enemy of everything that we have ever stood for. More than anybody else alive he has gone about to destroy tradition – to destroy us – to destroy our country. I suppose you realise what the effect of his last Budget is going to be when – when—'

'When I die. Yes, of course I do. It will mean the end of Warbeck Hall. I am sorry for you, Robert. You have had the misfortune to be born into the first generation of the dispossessed. I have been luckier. I can say of myself, in the old Latin phrase, that I am *Felix opportunitate mortis.* You can put that on my tombstone, if the Vicar will let you. But you know,' he went on, before Robert had time to speak, 'I think you are rather exaggerating the part Julius has played in this affair. After all, it would all have

28

happened in much the same way without him. He is only the figurehead of something far larger. In spite of all his posturings, I think he realises it from time to time, and then I find him rather a pathetic character.'

'Pathetic!' Robert was to be denied no longer. 'Shall I tell you what I think of him? He's nothing but a traitor to his class, a traitor to his country—'

'Don't shout, Robert. It's a nasty habit you've acquired from speaking at street corners. Besides, it's bad for me.'

'I'm sorry, Father.' Robert was all contrition at once. 'But I was never much good at forgiving my enemies.'

'"Enemies" is rather a strong word to use. I bear no ill will to Julius. He is, like the rest of us, in the power of what Dr Bottwink would call the *Zeitgeist*.'

'Bottwink? Who on earth is he?'

'Oh, an interesting little man. You'll see him directly. He's doing research work in the muniment room. Hardly your type, perhaps, but I like him.'

'He sounds like a Jew,' Robert said disgustedly.

'I have never asked him, but I shouldn't be at all surprised if he was. Does it matter? But perhaps I shouldn't have asked you that.'

Robert remained silent for a moment and then uttered a mirthless laugh. 'Really, it's a bit funny,' he said. 'I come down to Warbeck for Christmas, and find myself sharing it with Julius and a Jew boy! We ought to make a merry party!'

'I am sorry you take it like this, my dear boy,' said Lord Warbeck seriously. 'As a matter of fact, Dr Bottwink's presence is quite accidental. But your society won't be confined entirely to them. We can't afford much hospitality in these days, but we can do better than that.'

With the air of a man resigned to hear the worst, Robert said, 'I see. And who makes the rest of the house-party?'

'I'm hardly in a condition to entertain a house-party, Robert, even if the house was. As I told you, this is simply a last reunion of the family circle. There are not many people left who qualify under that head. First, of course, there is Mrs Carstairs—'

Robert groaned. 'Mrs Carstairs!' he said. 'I might have known it!'

'Your mother's oldest friend, Robert. She was also your poor brother's godmother, if I recollect rightly. I should have felt ashamed not to invite her.'

'What does it matter what she was? It's what she is that I object to. She's Alan Carstairs' wife, and all she's concerned with is pushing that dirty politician up the dirty political ladder. Also, she's a crashing bore,' he added.

'Well,' said Lord Warbeck resignedly, 'let us be thankful that the dirty politician is abroad and won't be here to trouble you. There is just one other guest,' he went on. 'I hope you will regard her as some compensation for the others.'

Robert's cheek glowed red in the firelight. He bit his lip and there was a distinct pause before he turned to look at his father.

'Camilla?' he asked.

'Yes, Camilla. I hope you're pleased.'

'I – I haven't seen her for some time.'

'So I gather. I hoped that would be all the more reason for your being glad to see her on this occasion.'

'It was nice of you to think of me, Father.'

'I've had a good deal of leisure for thinking lately.

It's one of the advantages that invalids have over normal people. And you – and Camilla – have been in my thoughts a good deal.'

Robert remained silent.

'I love that girl,' his father went on softly. 'She is very fond of you, unless I'm much mistaken. I used to think that you were fond of her. You've changed a lot in the last year or two, but I hoped you hadn't changed in that. I'm not such an old fogey as to think that parents can order their children's lives nowadays, but it would be a great comfort to me if before I go I could know that your future was assured. Why don't you ask her, Robert? Make this a happy Christmas for the two of you, and leave me to cope with the rest of the party!'

Robert did not reply at first. He had lighted a cigarette and was nervously flicking the ash into the fire.

'Look here, Father,' he said at last, 'I've been wanting to talk to you about – about this business for some time, but it's difficult. I—'

He stopped abruptly as the door opened and Briggs came into the room.

'Shall I serve tea, my lord?' he said.

'I said we would wait for the ladies, Briggs.'

'They are just arrived, my lord. They were delayed by the snow, I understand.'

'Then we'll have tea at once. Let Sir Julius know, and ask Dr Bottwink if he would care to join us.'

'Very good, my lord. I think I hear the ladies coming now.'

He withdrew and returned a moment later to announce, 'Lady Camilla Prendergast and Mrs Carstairs.'

IV

Tea for Six

The room seemed to be suddenly full of women. The quiet, masculine atmosphere of the library, redolent of wood smoke and old calf bindings, was charged with a new, disturbing element, made up of feminine scents and sounds. Robert felt that he and his father had dwindled into an insignificant minority. It was difficult to realise that in fact there were only two women present, and, moreover, that one of them was noticeably quiet. But any failure in self-assertion on her part was more than made up by her companion.

Friendly accounts of the activities of Mrs Carstairs were apt to contain somewhere the phrase that she was, would be, or had been 'a host in herself'; and the description had been taken up and applied by other commentators, not so friendly. It certainly fitted her invasion of Lord Warbeck's library. She overran it like an occupying army, distributing her fire right and left and reducing the inhabitants to a stunned quiescence.

'Dear Lord Warbeck!' she exclaimed as she swept in. 'How marvellous to be back in the dear old place again! It is really too good of you to think of asking me, especially when you've been so poorly – but you are better now, are you not? I had had such bad accounts of you that really at one time I was positively *anxious*. When I got your letter inviting me, I could hardly believe it at first, but I might have known – it was so like you not to forget old friends, even if our ways have lain apart these many years. Oh, Robert, dear boy, how are you? One can see with half an eye that you are well enough. Dear, dear, I'm afraid *our* ways have diverged with a vengeance! Never mind, we'll try and forget sore subjects, just for Christmas, shall we? Christmas ought to be a time for forgetting as well as for remembering, I always think. Oh, let me get near this lovely fire and thaw myself! I'm quite frozen!'

Somewhere in this monologue Lord Warbeck had contrived to interject a question as to her journey.

'Dreadful, dreadful! If I hadn't had the prospect of dear Warbeck to cheer me, I don't know how I could have borne it. The train was late, of course, and cold! It almost took me back to the bad old days before nationalisation – but I expect that in those days we should never have got through at all! And then we had a fiendish drive here. Really, on Telegraph Hill the snow was so thick we began to wonder if we would ever make it. Luckily the driver was a most sensible young man and he had chains and he—'

Decidedly, the room was full of women. But it was not Mrs Carstairs, despite her chatter, whose personality counted for most there. While the flow of trivialities went remorselessly on, Camilla Prendergast stepped quietly up to the sofa and bent over Lord Warbeck. There was a quick exchange of barely audible words, a kiss given and returned, and then she straightened herself and came across to Robert. He was standing by the window, his handsome face a non-committal mask.

'Well, Robert, how are you?'

'Oh, well, thank you. Are you well?'

'Yes, thanks.'

In the pause that followed Mrs Carstairs had time to carry her story all the way from the top of Telegraph Hill to the snowdrifts in Tangley Bottom. Then Camilla gave a little laugh.

'There doesn't seem to be much else to say, does there?'

'No, there doesn't.'

She looked over his shoulder at the window. Large flakes of snow were flattening themselves on the panes.

'Look at the snow!' she said. 'It's coming down as if it would never stop. Robert, has it occurred to you that it would be pretty bloody if we were cooped up here for days and days, with nothing to say but "How are you?"'

Robert did not look at the snow. Instead, he was looking very hard at Camilla. He grinned suddenly, but whether his amusement was genuine or not it was hard to tell.

'Quite bloody,' he said.

The appearance of Briggs with the tea-things brought the conversation – if such it could be called – to an end. Hard on his heels came Sir Julius, rubbing his hands and oozing geniality.

'Tea!' he exclaimed, with the air of someone confronted with an unexpected treat. 'Ah, splendid! It's what one needs on a cold day like this!'

'I hope you have finished grinding the faces of the rich for the day, Julius,' said Lord Warbeck. 'There's no need for me to introduce you to anybody here, I fancy.'

'Introduce me!' exclaimed Sir Julius with exaggerated surprise. 'I should think not. Camilla, my dear, you are looking more lovely than ever!'

'Thank you! Do you know, I was beginning to be afraid nobody would notice it.'

'My dear young lady, I can't believe that anyone would be so blind! If I were only a little younger, I— Ah, Mrs Carstairs! This is indeed a pleasure! We meet most appropriately. I have just been reading a masterly state paper from a certain gentleman in Washington – most masterly, I give you my word. You husband is doing a great work for us out there. He has really surprised us all.'

'He has not surprised *me*, Sir Julius.' Mrs Carstairs took him up with some asperity. 'I've known for some time that he has the best financial brain in Parliament – in the country, I may say – even if—'

'Even if – eh?' Sir Julius's good humour was quite unruffled. 'Even if – shall we say – a certain person is Chancellor of the Exchequer and Mr Carstairs is not? Never mind, his time will come. Every dog has his day, and we are all mortal. Tell him not to be impatient. That's the golden rule in politics.'

Something very like a chuckle came from the direction of the window embrasure and Sir Julius turned quickly in its direction.

'Ah, Robert,' he said, in a distinctly colder tone. 'I hadn't seen you there in the window. How are you?'

'How do you do?' replied Robert, equally coldly.

'You've only just arrived, I take it?'

'Yes. I had an important meeting in London yesterday.'

'Quite. The League of Liberty and Justice, I suppose?'

'And suppose it was? Is that any concern of yours?'

'I think it is the concern of every thinking man or woman in this country who cares for democracy.'

35

'And I think that what you are pleased to call democracy—'

'Camilla, I don't think you have met Dr Bottwink.' Lord Warbeck's quiet voice cut across the altercation. 'He has been good enough to spend his time rummaging among the papers here. Dr Bottwink, let me present you to Lady Camilla Prendergast – Mrs Carstairs – my son Robert. Sir Julius you have met already. And now, I think, our little party is complete. We are not likely to have anyone dropping in on a day like this. Draw the curtains, Briggs. Camilla, will you pour out tea for us?'

The tension was relaxed. As she busied herself with the teapot and the monumental silver urn that Briggs had thought appropriate to the occasion, Camilla found a half-forgotten nonsense rhyme coming into her head:

They put on the kettle, and little by little
They all became happy again.

For the moment at least, all was peace. The sight of the sugar-bowl had prompted Mrs Carstairs to engage Sir Julius in a technical discussion about the duties on colonial cane sugar. Robert was deep in conversation with his father on some equally innocuous topic. She found Dr Bottwink standing meekly beside her.

'Perhaps I should serve Lord Warbeck with his tea?' he suggested. 'The rest of the gathering would appear to be occupied.'

He fumbled with the cup she handed to him and almost dropped it.

'I must apologise for my clumsiness,' he said gravely,

'but the truth is, my fingers are a little numb.'

He delivered Lord Warbeck's tea safely, and returned. Camilla noticed that Robert disregarded his existence with almost insolent ostentation. Deliberately she set herself to be polite to this forlorn little man.

'Have you been working in the muniment room without a fire?' she asked. 'You must be perished!'

'One does not easily perish merely of cold, so long as food is available,' replied Dr Bottwink didactically. 'Such, at least, is my experience. But it is chilly. Scientists tell us of the existence of a condition known as absolute cold, and I am inclined to think that the muniment room is not so very far removed from that state.'

'You speak English very well,' said Camilla absently. She was looking past him towards Robert. With perverse pleasure she saw that he was scowling in her direction, as though her friendly attitude towards this foreigner annoyed him. 'He takes that amount of interest in me, anyway,' she thought. She could not resist the impulse of annoying him further. Breaking into his conversation with his father, she said:

'Uncle Tom, Dr Bottwink is telling me about absolute cold. Do you know what that is?'

'No, Camilla, but I am sure that it is something extremely disagreeable.'

'It seems to be rather like the muniment room.'

'I am sorry,' Lord Warbeck said civilly, turning to the historian. 'I am afraid it is difficult nowadays to make my guests as comfortable as I should wish.'

'Indeed, Lord Warbeck, I assure you, it is nothing. I should not have spoken as I did, even as a joke. I have been

37

many times much colder, and I repeat, it is nothing.' Dr Bottwink was pink with embarrassment.

For the first time Robert addressed him directly.

'No doubt you have found it colder in your own country,' he said slowly. 'What is your country, may I ask?'

In the face of his studied rudeness Dr Bottwink became perfectly calm again.

'That would be a little difficult to say exactly,' he replied. 'By nationality, I have been Austrian and Czech and German – in that order. But I am a bit Russian also, and it so happens that I was born in Hungary. So there are a good many ingredients in my make-up.'

'Including Jewish ingredients, I suppose?'

'Of course,' said Dr Bottwink, with a polite smile.

'Dr Bottwink, I wonder if I might trouble you to hand me those little cakes over there,' Lord Warbeck interposed. 'Thank you. You have no idea how much I have grown to envy people who can take their meals sitting up. Feeding lying down is the most messy business I know.'

Camilla adjusted the cushions behind his back.

'Poor Uncle Tom!' she said. 'Does this mean that you won't be able to dine with us this evening?'

'Yes, Camilla, it does. I shall, I trust, be asleep long before you have seen Christmas in. Robert will be your host on my behalf. I hope you don't mind.'

Camilla looked at Robert. He flushed slightly and avoided her eye.

'I hope Robert doesn't,' she said sweetly. 'Mrs Carstairs, can I give you another cup of tea?'

'Thank you, dear, so long as it's not too strong. As I was

saying, Sir Julius, my husband feels very strongly that the colonial sugar producer—'

'Lord Warbeck,' Dr Bottwink said diffidently, 'I wonder whether, in all the circumstances, it might perhaps be preferable if I did not accept your kind invitation to take dinner with your family this evening? It seems to me that possibly—'

'Nonsense, my dear fellow,' said his lordship kindly. 'I insist that you should. You are to consider yourself a guest of the house, just like anybody else.'

'But—'

'Of course you must dine with us,' Camilla put in. 'I shan't have anybody to talk to if you don't. Some more tea, Robert?' she added, with an innocent air.

'No, thank you,' said Robert emphatically. He rose to his feet. 'If I'm to preside over this festive affair tonight, I'd better have a word with Briggs about what we're going to drink.'

He stalked out of the room.

An awkward pause followed his departure. Mrs Carstairs, whose exposition of the problem of colonial sugar had temporarily exhausted itself, watched him go with an expression of shocked disapproval. Lord Warbeck's face was an angry red, Dr Bottwink's very pale. Camilla's hand trembled, so that she set down her cup with a clatter that sounded loud in the sudden silence. Only Sir Julius, deeply occupied in masticating plum cake, seemed unaware that anything out of the way had occurred.

Lord Warbeck was the first to speak. He was breathing heavily, and articulated with difficulty.

'I – I am sorry,' he contrived to say. 'My only son – a

guest in my house – I am ashamed—'

'Do not distress yourself, my lord, I beg of you,' Dr Bottwink said swiftly, his English becoming more formal than ever under the stress of the occasion. 'I comprehend the position perfectly. This regrettable little incident was only to be expected. It serves to confirm me in my opinion that I should absent myself from dinner this evening. Indeed, I indicated as much to your good Briggs yesterday. It is not that I do not appreciate your hospitality, but where matters of politics are concerned—'

'No politics in this house,' said Lord Warbeck feebly.

'Come here a moment,' said Camilla firmly. 'I want to talk to you.' She took the bewildered Bottwink by the arm and led him to the further end of the room. 'Look,' she said, 'I know exactly how you're feeling about this, but you've simply got to help us see this evening through. It's going to be pretty bloody anyhow, but without you it will only be worse, with Robert in his present mood.'

'Worse, Lady Camilla? I do not understand. How could it be worse, seeing that it is I who am the offender in his eyes?'

'Oh, don't imagine that you are the only one! You were merely the excuse for his bad manners. He hates Sir Julius every bit as much – more, I should say, because he thinks he is one of his own clan who has gone over to the other side. And he can't stand Mrs Carstairs either, for the same reason.'

'And you, my lady? Does he hate you also? And for what reason, if so?'

'That,' said Camilla slowly, 'is what I came down here to find out.'

'I comprehend you.'

'Thanks. I thought you would. You seem a – a comprehending sort of person.'

Dr Bottwink was silent for a moment. Then, looking towards the sofa, he said, 'It would distress Lord Warbeck, would it not, if I were to refuse?'

'It would upset him very much. This party was entirely his idea, and he's not likely to have another.'

Dr Bottwink sighed. 'I owe a great deal to his lordship,' he said. 'I will join your party this evening, Lady Camilla.'

'Thank you. I am really grateful for that.'

'All the same,' he continued ruefully, 'I fear that at the best I shall be somewhat of a fish out of water. Apart from being the object of Mr Robert's displeasure, there is so little in common between me and my fellow guests.'

'I'm sure you could get on with anyone.'

Dr Bottwink shook his head.

'It is not so,' he said. 'I am a man of rather specialised attainments. I had looked forward to meeting your Chancellor of the Exchequer, because there were certain points of constitutional theory and history affecting his office on which I fancied he could enlighten me. But when I broached the subject at breakfast I found him most unresponsive – indeed, I should have said ignorant.'

Camilla laughed. 'That was very simple of you, Dr Bottwink,' she said. 'Did you really expect a Cabinet Minister to know the first thing about constitutional history? He's much too busy running his department to bother about a thing like that.'

'I fear that my knowledge of England is still imperfect,' said the historian mildly. 'On the Continent it used not

41

to be uncommon to find professors of history in Cabinet posts.'

'Well, it's no good thinking you'll make the party go by trying to cross-examine Julius about the British constitution,' said Camilla firmly. 'He hates talking shop, anyhow. Didn't you see how Mrs Carstairs was boring him just now about the sugar duties? No, if you want to draw him out, try golf or fishing. Those are the only subjects he's really keen about.'

'Golf and fishing,' echoed Dr Bottwink gravely. 'Thank you, Lady Camilla. I shall remember. Perhaps with your assistance I shall even understand English public life at last!'

V

Robert in the Toils

Robert closed the door of the library behind him and stepped out into the corridor with a sigh of relief. To reach the servants' quarters he would have had to turn to his left, but instead, after a moment's hesitation, he walked in the opposite direction. He had not taken more than a few paces before he stopped in surprise. A man was standing near the wall at a corner of the corridor, apparently engaged in earnest contemplation of an equestrian portrait of the sixth Lord Warbeck as master of the Mid-Markshire foxhounds. The stranger was neatly dressed in a grey tweed suit and contrived to be at once very large and quite unobtrusive. He appeared to be quite at his ease, and at Robert's approach moved to one side to let him pass with the air of one who expected his presence to be taken for granted.

Robert was in no mood to take anything or anybody for granted. His Christmas at Warbeck, he felt, was becoming a whole series of disagreeable surprises. The presence of yet another unexpected guest was the last straw.

'And who the devil may you be?' he asked truculently.

'The name, sir, is Rogers,' the large man replied civilly. There was something oddly impersonal about his voice, as though it came from a particularly well-bred machine.

'What are you doing, hanging about here?'

'Well, sir, hanging about is my job, in a manner of speaking. My card, sir.'

A small, square card materialised suddenly in his hand, and Robert found himself reading:

METROPOLITAN POLICE. SPECIAL BRANCH.

James Arthur Rogers holds the rank of sergeant in the Metropolitan Police. This is his warrant and authority for executing the duties of his office.

'I see.' He handed the card back to its owner, holding it between his finger-tips as though its very touch was distasteful. 'So you're one of those, are you? Haven't I seen you before, some time?'

'Yes, sir. On Sunday, September twentieth last, between the hours of 8 and 10 p.m.'

'Eh?'

'Open-air meeting, League of Liberty and Justice, sir. I was on duty.'

'That explains it. And now they've sent you down here to continue your spying, I suppose?'

'Oh no, sir. I'm here on protection duty – looking after Sir Julius.'

Robert threw back his head and laughed out loud.

'Protection!' he said. 'That's rich! He needs it! I can tell you this, my man, and you can tell your superiors when you get back to Scotland Yard: when our movement gets into power, fellows like you are going to be out of a job.'

'Oh no, sir,' the detective replied imperturbably. 'That's just what Sir Julius's friends used to say in the old days when I attended their meetings. You'll want protection just the same. They all do.'

A discreet cough behind him made Robert turn round abruptly.

'Excuse me, sir.' Briggs spoke respectfully enough, but his look was disapproving. Evidently, a colloquy between the son of the house and a policeman was not one of the things provided for in the traditions of Warbeck Hall. He turned to Sergeant Rogers. 'Your tea is awaiting you in the housekeeper's room, Mr Rogers,' he said briskly.

'Thank you, Mr Briggs.'

'Don't let me keep you, Sergeant,' said Robert, pointedly.

'I am much obliged to you, sir,' Rogers replied with unabashed good humour, and took himself off.

Robert watched him go with a look of disgust.

'This is what we have to put up with nowadays, Briggs,' he observed.

'Quite, sir.' The butler coughed again. 'Pardon me, Mr Robert, but would it be convenient for me to have a word with you now?'

Robert turned and looked at him without speaking. Briggs remained in the deferential attitude that years of training had imposed upon him, but his eyes met and held those of his master's son without flinching, and in the end it was Robert who looked away.

In the same respectful tones, Briggs went on, 'I have lighted a fire in the smoking-room, sir. Perhaps that would be most convenient.'

Still without a word, Robert strode down the passage, passed through the door which Briggs held open for him, and threw himself into an armchair by the smoking-room fire. The butler remained, as a butler should, standing squarely in the centre of the carpet while Robert, his long legs stretched out in front of him, stared moodily at the toes of his shoes. The silence became oppressive, until Robert could bear it no longer. Looking up, he barked out suddenly, 'Well, Briggs? Why don't you say something?'

'I was hoping, sir, that some suggestion would come from you.'

'I have no suggestion to make.'

'In that case, sir, you must allow me to point out that my daughter Susan is now—'

'Look here, Briggs!' Robert was on his feet now. His splendidly athletic form towered over the submissive figure standing before him. 'What on earth is the good of bringing up all this business again now? You know what the position is as well as I do. We have been into it time and time again. I should have thought that you of all people would be able to trust me. I have promised you before, and I can promise you now—'

'Promises are all very well, Mr Robert,' said the butler steadily. 'But that was some time ago, and there are now two persons to consider, not counting myself. It is high time that something was done.'

'Do you really imagine that this is a suitable time to do something, as you put it – with my father dangerously ill and the house full of people? You're being utterly unreasonable, Briggs. Things must go on as they are for the time being. When I have an opportunity to talk to my father, I will.'

'I am afraid that is not altogether satisfactory, sir.'

'Briggs!' Robert's tone became menacing. 'Are you trying to threaten me?'

'I should not like to put it that way, sir.'

'This is a matter between myself and Susan. She is of age, and perfectly capable of looking after herself. If she was not satisfied with the present position, she would be here to say so.'

'She is here, sir,' said Briggs calmly.

'Here?' Robert was visibly staggered. 'Do you mean to tell me that she is actually here now – in this house?'

'Precisely, sir.'

Robert said nothing for a full half-minute. Then he said in the tone of a man admitting defeat, 'She wants to see me, I suppose?'

'No, sir.' Briggs might have been discussing the choice of a liqueur to serve after dinner for all the emotion he displayed. 'She feels a certain embarrassment in her present situation in seeing anybody. That is one reason why she feels – we feel – that it would be desirable for the position to be clarified as soon as possible.'

'I see – I see.' Robert's voice became harsh again. 'And you brought her here with the object of applying a little extra pressure, eh? A very pretty piece of blackmail, Briggs, upon my word.'

'Blackmail is a term that I should deprecate, sir.'

'What else is it? You have no other excuse I know of for letting her into this house.'

'Well, sir,' said Briggs, showing a trace of feeling for the first time, 'Christmas is the season for family reunions, I understand – even for butlers. So far as applying pressure is concerned, I trust that that will not become necessary. We are still relying upon you to act in every way as becomes a gentleman.'

The word 'gentleman' had in Briggs's mouth a force and simplicity that left Robert momentarily speechless. Perhaps only a man in that station of life could have used it in precisely that way. Himself by definition not a gentleman, but sworn to the service of gentility, he was appealing to the standard under which he and his fellows had lived out their lives, and without which that service would have been degraded to mere servitude.

Angry and alarmed though he was, Robert felt something of the deep feeling that informed the butler's quiet words. It was with an effort that he brought the discussion back to a practical level.

'You said just now that Susan didn't want to see anyone. But surely the other servants in the house—'

'I have been compelled to take the cook and the head housemaid into my confidence, sir, but only to a limited extent. They are aware that she is my daughter, but no more. I have allowed the impression to circulate that she is a widow. Greatly though I regret the necessity of subterfuge, sir, it seemed to be the best course.'

'I see . . . Briggs, I must think this over. I shall—'

A faint tinkling sound in the distance cut across his halting phrases. Briggs was on the alert at once. He had been listening to Robert with strained attention, but now he cut him short without ceremony.

'Excuse me, sir. I think that is his lordship's bell.'

He went to the door. Just as he reached for the handle, it was opened from without and Camilla appeared in the entrance. He only just stopped himself in time to avoid walking right into her. Pink with embarrassment, he stepped back, murmuring, 'I beg your ladyship's pardon. I had no idea—'

'That's all right, Briggs,' said Camilla rather breathlessly. 'His lordship wants you to help him upstairs. He's decided to go to bed.'

'Very good, my lady.'

Briggs vanished with the unhurried speed that is the trade secret of butlers, and Camilla turned to Robert.

'Give me a cigarette,' she said abruptly.

Robert extended his cigarette case and provided her with a light. Camilla stood by the fire, one foot on the low fender, one hand on the mantelpiece, looking downwards into the flames. It was an attractive pose and the flickering light of the burning logs gave colour and movement to features which a connoisseur might ordinarily have thought a trifle too cold and impassive. If Robert noticed the effect, he was careful not to show that he had done so. He waited until the cigarette was half consumed before he broke the silence.

'I thought Father meant to stay up longer,' he said. 'He's not feeling ill or anything, is he?'

'No, he's all right. He only complained of feeling tired.'

'I don't wonder he's tired, if he's been listening to Julius and the Carstairs woman talking about sugar.'

'He stood it longer than you did, anyway, Robert,' said Camilla with a faint grin.

The conversation dropped again and Robert showed no disposition to revive it. Finally Camilla threw the butt of her cigarette into the fire and turned towards him.

49

'Well?' she asked. 'And how did the discussion with Briggs go off?'

'Discussion?' Robert was on the defensive at once. 'What do you mean? What should I be having a discussion with him about?'

'About the wine for dinner tonight,' Camilla said with an air of innocent surprise. 'I thought it was that that dragged you away from tea so reluctantly.'

'Oh – that. Yes, the drink's laid on all right.'

'I hope there's enough of it, that's all,' said Camilla in a sudden vicious little outburst. 'I mean to drink a lot tonight. I mean to get positively, completely blotto.'

'That will add enormously to your attractions.'

'Well, they want adding to, don't they? I mean, they don't seem to have been very effective so far.'

'On the contrary, Julius paid you a very pretty compliment, and your new Jew friend seemed to be quite overcome. Has he asked you to go back to Palestine with him yet?'

'Poor Robert!'

'I didn't know that I was in any need of pity.'

'Don't you? Perhaps not – and that makes you all the more pitiful. You used to be rather a sweet person, you know, and now you've gone sour and bitter. What's happened?'

'Nothing, so far as I am aware.'

'Robert, that's nonsense. A man can't change in the way you have done and not know that anything's happened to him.'

'I don't see where the change comes in. I never did like Jews or socialists and I don't like them now.'

Camilla sighed impatiently. 'Can't we keep politics out of it?' she asked.

'By all means. I never asked you to bring them in, did I?'

'I don't mind about your League of Liberty and Justice—'

'That's very good of you. I'll tell them when I get back to London. They'll be tremendously relieved.'

Camilla brushed the interruption aside.

'You can be any damned thing you please, so long as it *is* you, and not this awful, cynical caricature of yourself,' she persisted.

'You're talking nonsense!'

'Robert!' Camilla caught him by the sleeve. 'Robert! Look at me! We've known each other pretty well all our lives – since we were children. It's no use trying to pretend to me that nothing's the matter, when anyone can see with half an eye that you're miserably unhappy! Won't you – won't you let me help you, Robert? It's not much to ask, is it? We used to be such friends – I – I'd do anything to help you. D'you understand what I mean, Robert? Anything! I simply can't stand going on like this. Look at me, for God's sake, look at me!'

'Let go of me, Camilla,' said Robert through clenched teeth. 'I warn you, let go!'

'Not until you've told me what has happened. Say you hate me if you like, only let me know why. God knows, I don't want to do anything to hurt you. I simply want to help. I want – I want—'

'You want, you want!' Robert had rounded on her suddenly. His powerful hands gripped her arms, his face was within a few inches of hers. 'I know what you want, all right! There's no need to be so mealy-mouthed about it. You want a man. That's what you came down here for, wasn't it? All right, now's your chance. Would you like me to lock the door now and turn out the light? I dare say we could make do on the sofa.'

'Robert, you're hurting me! Let go!'

'Or perhaps you'd rather wait till tonight, when you've had a skinful of champagne to overcome your maidenly reserve? You said just now that you meant to get blotto, didn't you? I dare say that'll be best, and I can have a drop too to make things even. D'you think you can wait till then?'

'You're mad, Robert! For heaven's sake, leave go of me!'

'That's a bargain, then, my pretty. One of us will have a happy Christmas, at any rate. And just to remind you before you go—'

He kissed her three or four times, violently, brutally, crushing her lips with his.

'That will be all for now,' he said as he released her. 'I hope you're satisfied?'

Pale with anger, Camilla staggered away from him.

'Oh, you're hateful, hateful!' she sobbed. 'You filthy beast. I could kill you for this!'

With the flat of her hand she caught him a violent blow on the face, and before he could move again had run from the room.

VI

Company in the Pantry

The butler's pantry at Warbeck Hall was, as Dr Bottwink had pointed out to Briggs, part of the original building, whether the mythical Perkin had been responsible for its construction or no. At some period a portion of what had been in medieval times the main living-room of the house had been partitioned off to form a narrow oblong chamber, disproportionately high for its width. Only the stone-flagged floor and the tiny lancet windows cut in the massive outer wall remained to vouch for its antiquity. Its sides were lined with cupboards and shelves, on which were arranged with meticulous care silver, glasses, cleaning materials and all the apparatus of civilisation as a butler sees it. Here was Briggs's domain – cold, austere and scrupulously clean – and here, having put his master to bed, Briggs, in his shirtsleeves, a baize apron tied round his ample waist, was engaged in the absorbing task of polishing the spoons and forks for the evening's dinner. The light from a naked electric bulb gleamed on his bald head. His breath steamed on the chilly air, heavy with the smell of plate polish.

He had been working for some time when the door behind him opened silently and the head of a young woman appeared behind it. She had a pretty, if undistinguished, face, disfigured by an anxious expression which had permanently depressed the corners of her mouth. Her fiery red hair glowed in contrast to the pallor of her cheeks. After a pause for observation, the newcomer finally entered the room and walked quietly up to the table where the butler was standing.

'Dad!' she breathed softly. 'Dad!'

Without turning round or pausing for an instant in his work, Briggs said, 'You had no call to come down here, Susan my girl. You'll catch your death of cold. I told you to stay upstairs by your fire.'

'I'm sorry, Dad, but I couldn't wait to see you. Have you – have you spoken to him, Dad?'

'Yes, I've spoken to him all right.'

'What did he say? What's he going to do about it?'

Briggs held a Georgian fish-slice up to the light, breathed on it and rubbed it vigorously with a piece of shammy-leather before replying.

'That I can't say exactly. We were interrupted before we could get that far. But something's got to be done, and done soon. I put that to him straight.'

'Oh, what's the good of saying things like that?' the girl burst out petulantly. 'That means you've let him get away with it again, and now he'll go on wriggling and wriggling and putting things off, the same as he's done before.'

'All the same, I don't think he will this time,' said Briggs, grimly, apparently addressing himself to the saltspoon in his hand.

'I've a good mind to go straight off and tell his lordship,' Susan continued. 'That would make him sit up!'

'None of that now, my girl!' The butler spun round on his heels and faced his daughter for the first time. So fierce was his aspect that she recoiled from him involuntarily.

'I'm sorry, Dad,' she faltered. 'I didn't mean it, really.'

'I should hope you didn't. I haven't been in this house forty-five years to be the cause of giving his lordship a shock that might send him to his grave. And if your poor mother was alive she'd say the same.'

'Is he as ill as all that?'

'I don't suppose there's anybody beyond me and his lordship that knows how ill he is,' said Briggs seriously. 'It only wants a proper shock for him to go off like – that.' He snapped his fingers, and then turned back to his work.

'It's funny, though, isn't it?' Susan observed to her father's back. 'I mean, him being there and me here. It's not fair, is it? After all, I've got my rights, the same as anyone else, haven't I?'

'You've got your rights, my girl, and in good time you'll get your rights,' Briggs assured her. 'Now you cut along upstairs.'

Susan retreated, but stopped half-way to the door.

'Dad?'

'What is it now?'

'Is it true that me and him are – sort of cousins, in a way?'

The butler turned round once more and looked at her in silence for a moment.

'Someone's been telling tales,' he said finally.

'Well, are we?'

'You've got the colour for it,' said Briggs, his eyes on his daughter's hair. 'And more than that I will not say. Your mother's great-auntie used to drop hints about goings-on in the sixth viscount's days, but I never paid any attention to them, and my advice to you is to do the same. You've enough on your plate already. But if the idea gives you some sort of fellow feeling with his lordship, I've no objection. Off with you now! I don't want anyone to come in and find you here.'

Susan vanished, and Briggs, his work completed, began arranging the silver on a tray. He was checking it over when the pantry door opened again.

'Oh, Briggs, I am sorry to bother you.' It was Camilla, her face rather flushed, her manner unusually disturbed.

'Not at all, my lady. Were you requiring anything?' said Briggs, hastily removing his apron and assuming his coat.

'Yes. It's so stupid of me, I find I've forgotten to pack a shoe-horn. I know you keep every kind of treasure here. Have you got such a thing, I could borrow?'

'A shoe-horn, my lady?' Briggs considered for a moment. 'Yes, I think I could find you one.'

He pulled open the door of one of the cupboards, and almost at once produced an elegantly made silver shoe-horn, which he polished with his leather before handing it to her.

'What a lovely little thing!' Camilla exclaimed. 'Where does it come from?'

'A coming-of-age present to his late lordship,' Briggs explained. 'I don't suppose it has ever been used.'

'You are a marvel, Briggs. How on earth do you know where everything is?'

'I've lived with them a long time, my lady. I arranged these shelves when I was a pantry-boy, and I suppose I could lay my hands on anything.'

Camilla walked the length of the room, throwing open one cupboard after another.

'Marvellous!' she repeated. 'It doesn't look as though a thing has changed since I used to come in here and interrupt you in your work when I was a child.'

'There's certainly no silver missing since then, my lady, and not much glass broken either.'

'It's a lovely display. Are those Queen Anne forks, Briggs?'

'William and Mary, my lady . . . Would you excuse me, my lady, but I've got to take these things through to the dining-room to lay the table.'

'Of course, Briggs. I've been interrupting you again, just as I used to. What time is dinner?'

'Eight o'clock, my lady.'

'I needn't go up to dress yet awhile, then. Can you trust me not to steal any silver if I poke about here a little? I'd forgotten how fascinating it all was.'

'That will be all right, of course, my lady,' said Briggs, as he picked up the heavy tray. He paused at the door to say, 'Your ladyship mentioned dressing for dinner. If I may venture to say so, a sleeveless dress is not recommended for this evening. The dining-room, I fear, will be somewhat chilly.'

When he returned to the pantry, a quarter of an hour later, Lady Camilla had gone, but the servants' quarters were still not free of invasion from the other side of the house. Along the stone-flagged passage that led to the kitchen he could hear the clack of high-heeled shoes, and Mrs Carstairs' voice floated towards him.

'Dear Warbeck!' he heard. 'Forgive me, cook, but I couldn't resist poking my nose in! I've been running simply all over the house, renewing old associations. Dear me! What a lot of good meals I've seen being cooked in this wonderful old kitchen of yours!'

From what he could hear of the murmured replies to Mrs Carstairs' advances, Briggs judged that her reception had been no more than barely civil. The cook, who was not, like himself, of the old régime, would be far too concerned with the exigencies of preparing Christmas Eve dinner on her antiquated range to welcome interruption. Before long, Mrs Carstairs gave up her attempts at fraternisation and returned the way she had come. She paused at the pantry door to give him the benefit of her presence.

'Oh, Briggs, I was just explaining to the cook, I've been on the prowl all over this dear old house! And really, you know, I think you people have the best of it. There's an atmosphere of antiquity about this wing that is quite unique!'

'It is a very cold atmosphere in this weather, madam,' said the butler unsympathetically.

'Yes, yes, of course, I know it is. And some people feel cold so much more than others. But all the same, Briggs, you must admit that it is a privilege to work in the original Warbeck Hall, in a room actually built by Perkin Warbeck himself—'

'Ah no, madame, I must protest! That is a myth, put about by the makers of guide-books! It has no historical foundation whatever.'

The voice came from behind her and she turned in surprise.

'Mr Bottling! You gave me quite a shock!'

'Dr Bottwink is the name, madame.'

'Of course. I'm so stupid about names, I'm afraid,

especially foreign ones. I had no idea you were there. Where did you spring from?'

Dr Bottwink pointed upwards.

'From the muniment room,' he explained. 'It is immediately above our heads. This little staircase in the wall behind me communicates directly with it.'

'Why, yes! I had quite forgotten it. "Perkin's staircase" we used to call it. I suppose you would say that was wrong too?'

'I regret, madame, much as it must distress you and Briggs, it is quite wrong. None the less, this pantry is an interesting old piece of building. Did you know that there was just one little bit of the original linen-fold panelling left?'

'Really,' said Mrs Carstairs peevishly, 'I never thought I should have anything told me about Warbeck by a stranger. I really think you must be mistaken, Mr – er, Dr—'

'But it is there, none the less, madame. Just a little piece, at the back of that cupboard next to the sink. It is nothing to look at – it is badly damaged, and has been painted over many times in the last few centuries, but it is undoubtedly a genuine morsel of linen-fold panelling and coeval with the fabric of the house. If you are interested, I will show it to you now.'

'If it is in the state you describe, it's hardly worth while wasting time to look at it,' said Mrs Carstairs shortly.

'True, madame. It is of little interest – except that, unlike Perkin Warbeck, it is genuine.' And with this Parthian shot the historian withdrew.

'Really!' Mrs Carstairs was breathing heavily in indignation. 'This gentleman seems to have been making free with your pantry in a remarkable way, Briggs. It seems most uncalled for. Why, anything might happen in a room full of valuables like this.'

'Well, madam,' said Briggs tolerantly, 'one must make allowances. The gentleman is a foreigner, after all. He certainly has a craze for anything that's really old and out of date. He told me that was why he was so interested in the British constitution.'

'That's one thing foreigners will never understand,' said Mrs Carstairs emphatically. 'They imagine that we are still living in the past. They don't realise the great changes that have come over the country in the last few years and that there are greater ones still to come.'

'Quite, madam,' said Briggs, with a noticeable lack of enthusiasm.

'Dinner is at eight as usual, I suppose?'

'Yes, madam. The dressing gong will be sounded at half-past seven.'

The difference between Briggs's feelings for Mrs Carstairs and for Lady Camilla Prendergast might be gauged by the fact that he elected to let her go without any warning as to the probable temperature of the diningroom.

There was still a multitude of tasks to be performed before dinner was ready to be served. The butler's next move was to the cellar. He returned some five minutes later, tenderly bearing a bottle heavily encrusted with cobwebs, and his heart sank to see yet another visitor in the pantry. He sighed with relief when he saw that it was only Sergeant Rogers.

'Sorry to disturb you, Mr Briggs,' Rogers said, 'but have you seen my bloke anywhere about?'

'Sir Julius has not been here, so far as I am aware, Mr Rogers. He's about the only member of the house-party who has not.'

'Funny. He must have given me the slip somehow. I could have sworn I saw him making off in this direction. In a big house like this it's a job to keep an eye on people, don't you find, Mr Briggs?'

'Keeping an eye on people is not part of my duty, I am glad to say, Mr Rogers. I have plenty to do as it is.'

Briggs reached down a decanter from a shelf.

'Well,' said the detective philosophically, 'I dare say it will do him no harm to be by himself for a little. That is a nice-looking bottle of port you have there, Mr Briggs.'

'This,' said Briggs crushingly, 'is the last bottle but one of his lordship's 1878, if you want to know, Mr Rogers.'

'You don't say, Mr Briggs! Pre-phylloxera!'

Briggs looked at him with a sudden air of respect. 'You know something about port, then, Mr Rogers?' he asked.

'A little, Mr Briggs. Just a little.'

'In that case, Mr Rogers, perhaps you would be good enough to assist me with the decanting.'

'I shall be proud to do so, Mr Briggs,' said the detective. Then, as Briggs produced a corkscrew he said anxiously, 'Do you think the cork is altogether safe? I was wondering whether with a wine of this age it would be wiser to take the neck off the bottle?'

'Quite unnecessary, Mr Rogers. His late lordship had the bin recorked as recently as 1913, so I think we should have no difficulty.'

Briggs was right. The cork was drawn without incident and the precious fluid was decanted with a steady hand while Rogers held a candle beneath the neck of the bottle to detect the presence of any floating impurity.

'There!' said the butler, holding up the bottle when the rite had been accomplished. 'A beautiful crust, and not a teaspoonful of dregs left at the bottom. I am very much obliged to you, Mr Rogers.'

The two men looked in admiration at the decanter.

'His lordship will take a small glass with a biscuit,' murmured Briggs. 'The doctor wouldn't allow him that, if he knew. I doubt whether the party in the dining-room are good for half a bottle between them. It's wasted on the ladies, of course ... I think if you were to join me here after dinner, Mr Rogers, there should be a couple of glasses apiece.'

'Well, Mr Briggs,' said Rogers judicially, 'it would be interesting to see what its condition is after all this time.'

And on this note the two connoisseurs parted.

VII

Christmas Dinner

At ten minutes to eight Briggs carried a tray bearing a decanter of sherry and glasses into the drawing-room. At eight o'clock precisely he sounded the great Chinese gong in the hall. It was an entirely unnecessary piece of ritual, for he had already seen for himself that all five guests were present; but as a piece of ritual he enjoyed it. The deep brazen notes pulsated through the great, half-empty house, penetrating into dilapidated spare rooms where no guests had been since the First World War, rousing echoes in servants' quarters where no servant was ever likely to be seen again. Oddly enough, the one person who seemed to share Briggs's pleasure in the noise was Sir Julius, who was once more momentarily in the grip of the spell of the past.

'Wonderful tone, that old gong,' he observed to Lady Camilla. 'You can hear it right the other side of the park when the windows are open, I remember. There's nothing like Chinese work for that sort of thing. I remember my father telling me it came from the loot of the Winter Palace at Pekin. Great days! Great days!' He sipped his sherry appreciatively.

'Surely, Sir Julius, you don't suggest that the sack of the Winter Palace was a creditable episode in our history?' broke in Mrs Carstairs.

'My dear lady, I am merely stating the fact that the gong

came from the Winter Palace at Pekin,' said Sir Julius, rather irritably.

'Pardon,' said Dr Bottwink rather diffidently to Camilla, while an acrid discussion proceeded on the events surrounding the Boxer revolt of 1900, 'but from whatever quarter the instrument originated, am I not correct in thinking that it signifies dinner-time?'

'Oh, yes,' Camilla assured him. 'It signifies that all right.'

'Then why do we not obey the summons and make our way to the dining-room?'

'That would never do! Briggs hasn't announced dinner yet. He always allows three minutes.'

'I comprehend. Inasmuch as the language of a gong is liable to be ambiguous, being Chinese, it is necessary that it should be reinforced by an announcement made in plain English.'

'*Plain* English, Dr Bottwink?' Camilla could not resist saying. It was odd, she reflected, but of all the people present this stranger, with his odd pedantic utterances, was the only one to whom she could talk with any degree of ease. Julius was a pompous egoist, Mrs Carstairs was a plain bore, and Robert – she looked across the room to where he stood. He had drunk three glasses of sherry rapidly without exchanging a word with anyone and was now ostentatiously disregarding her.

'Plain English,' Dr Bottwink repeated. 'I know what you mean, Lady Camilla. It is a language, you would say, of which I am not entitled to speak. The language of Shakespeare and Johnson, that I have mastered perhaps. But what you call plain English – that series of grunts and variations on a single indeterminate vowel by which nine-tenths of the inhabitants of this island choose to communicate—'

'Dinner is served!' Briggs's solemn announcement saved the historian from the trouble of finding an end to a sentence which was rapidly getting out of hand.

'We'll go in, shall we?' said Robert, speaking for the first time.

The dinner table was a small island in the middle of the vast room, and the room was as cold as Briggs had predicted. The ill-assorted little company sat down to their meal in a subdued mood. Apart from taking the head of the table, Robert showed no disposition to do his duty as a host. He ate what was put before him, drank copiously and said nothing. His obvious boredom at the entire proceedings set the tone for what promised to be a remarkably cheerless Christmas dinner. Little by little, however, the influence of food and drink began to have its effect. Beginning with Mrs Carstairs, whose loquacity nothing could curb for long, the guests contrived to keep going a sporadic conversation. None the less, there was an atmosphere of constraint which it was difficult to shake off. The long gaps between the little outbursts of talk were filled with a chill sense of foreboding, not only to be accounted for by the physical temperature of the dining-room.

It was Dr Bottwink in the end who saved the situation, and caused the meal to close in something nearer animation than had at first seemed possible. Evidently remembering Camilla's advice, he contrived to ask Sir Julius a question about fly-fishing. The statesman looked at him with undisguised surprise. The funny little foreigner, his expression said, might almost be human.

'Are *you* a fisherman?' he asked incredulously.

'In my youth I was quite fond of the sport,' said Dr Bottwink mildly. 'There are some quite passable trout streams in my country – not,' he added deprecatingly, 'to be compared with your Markshire rivers, of course, but quite good in their way.'

'Interesting,' said Sir Julius, dismissing all the waters of central Europe with a shrug of his shoulders. 'I remember—'

Camilla sent a glance of gratitude towards the historian. Fishing, she knew, was a subject on which Sir Julius could be thoroughly boring, but at least it could be guaranteed to keep the oppressive silence at bay for several minutes at a time. She was not disappointed. Julius launched easily into a disquisition on the technicalities, difficulties and virtues of the sport, particularly from the point of view of the harassed statesman, seeking relaxation from his toils. He compared himself to the late Lord Grey, not wholly to that statesman's advantage, and illustrated his theme with a few personal experiences, as fascinating to his hearers as other people's fishing stories invariably are. While he was leaving his audience to reflect upon the singularity of one of these, Dr Bottwink, who seemed to have been following the discourse with rapt attention, observed, 'Fishing for trout closely resembles the conduct of a love affair, does it not?'

'Eh?' Sir Julius was evidently taken aback. Mrs Carstairs, who had been paying little attention to the monologue, stiffened abruptly. Even Robert looked up from his turkey and favoured Dr Bottwink with a stare.

'But has it never occurred to you, Sir Julius? The parallel has always seemed to my mind singularly exact. Consider.' He held up one hand, and ticked off his propositions on his

fingers. 'You will agree that in both cases you are put, to begin with, to the necessity of going to considerable trouble
and expense, and in particular the purchase of costly baits
and allurements, many of which will in the end prove quite
useless. Next, the stage of preparation completed, there follows – does there not? – the period of reverie, when on
the eve of the event you promise yourself unheard-of success and rapture. Third stage: the assignation is made –
at the water-side or elsewhere, as the case may be. Your
quarry is within reach, you suffer the delicious agony of
anticipation and uncertainty. Think next of the difficulties
and disappointments you may encounter, the fatal blunders
you may commit up to the very last moment when success
seems certain! Remember especially that whatever your
skill you may yet be defeated by the mere coyness and
reluctance of your prey unless you can bring to your task
just that combination of ardour and prudence which is the
special gift of the lover! And finally there is the supreme
moment of triumph! How exquisite – and how brief!'

He concluded his harangue by drinking off a glass of
champagne amid a sudden silence.

'Really!' exclaimed Mrs Carstairs. She had gone extremely pink and was sitting more stiffly upright than
ever.

Dr Bottwink looked at her in alarm. Had he, his expression said, offended yet again these incalculable English?
Averting his eyes from the spectacle of outraged virtue,
he said diffidently, 'I fear that you do not altogether agree
with my comparison, Sir Julius?'

'No,' said Julius, 'I don't.' A new light on his favourite
recreation had been suddenly vouchsafed to him, and for

a long moment it was a question whether he would be offended or amused. To give himself time he too took a glass of champagne, and the generous wine decided for him. 'Not altogether,' he continued. 'Because I have had the experience of catching half a dozen fish inside twenty minutes, and I've never heard of any man who—'

'Sir Julius!' trumpeted Mrs Carstairs, but there was an ominous break in her voice.

Camilla found herself laughing, more out of relief than anything else, and quite suddenly Robert joined in with a peal of laughter.

When, a few moments later, Briggs brought in the plum pudding, he found the party, as he reported to Rogers, 'as cheerful as you'd never believe'.

The good humour so unexpectedly acquired lasted until the end of the meal. By common consent the ladies remained in the dining-room after dessert, and saw the precious 1878 port being fearfully punished by Julius and still more by Robert. Briggs came in to enquire whether coffee should be served in the drawing-room. His face was taut with disapproval as he saw Robert empty the last drains of the decanter into his glass. Camilla noticed his expression, but misunderstood its cause. Robert had certainly drunk enough. From being very silent he had become extremely talkative. To some extent, it was a turn for the better. For the time being, there had been flashes of the Robert whom she had known in the past – witty, genial and companionable. He had rallied Sir Julius and Mrs Carstairs on their politics without offence, and even been civil to Dr Bottwink. But the line between being better for drink and worse for it is a narrow one. At any moment the line might be crossed and he might say or do something utterly unforgivable.

'Coffee in the drawing-room, I think,' said Robert. The last of the irrecoverable vintage slipped down his throat. 'And put out the card table. We might have a rubber of bridge.'

'Very good, Mr Robert.'

On the way to the drawing-room Dr Bottwink took Camilla aside.

'Perhaps this would be a good opportunity for me to retire, if you would excuse me,' he said. 'You will have your party of bridge without me, and I shall only be superfluous.'

'Nonsense,' said Camilla firmly. 'You can't desert us now. Besides—' She cast a glance in the direction of Robert, who was walking in front with the exaggerated care of the tipsy.

'He is a trifle intoxicated, of course,' said Dr Bottwink judicially. 'Do you think that my continued presence might be of use?'

'Be of use? My dear man, don't you realise that you completely saved the whole show at dinner?'

'Ah, that!' The historian smiled thinly. 'But that was easy. I merely put myself in mind of the famous dictum of Sir Robert Walpole on dinner-table conversation, and acted upon it.'

'It may be famous, but I've never heard of it. What did Sir Robert Walpole say?'

Dr Bottwink hesitated. 'Perhaps it would be improper for me to quote it,' he said. 'It is probably not included in young ladies' history books.'

VIII

The Last Toast

It was ten minutes to midnight. The last rubber of bridge had just come to an end — Sir Julius and Mrs Carstairs against Robert and Camilla. Dr Bottwink, who had cut out, was peering past the curtains out of the window. The snow, he could see, was still falling, implacably. He shivered, let the curtain fall back into place, and turned to survey the little group round the card table. Sir Julius, a cigar clenched between his teeth, was grunting audibly as he tried to add up the score. Opposite him, Mrs Carstairs was impatiently tapping the table, barely concealing her contempt at her partner's slowness. Camilla's face was half averted from him, but he could see that she was very pale. It struck him that her attitude was strangely tense and strained. She was looking across to where Robert sprawled in his chair, and Dr Bottwink guessed that could he have caught the expression on her face he would have seen there a look of anxiety and expectation. He looked at Robert in his turn. It was plain that the good humour induced by dinner had been no more than a transient mood. There was an air of truculence about him now, which had reflected itself in some increasingly wild and unsuccessful play during the last half-hour or so. A disregarded spectator in the shadows, Dr Bottwink gazed at him with cold and steady dislike, remembering other men who had professed principles not so very different from those of the League of Liberty and Justice, who had been noisy and genial in their cups, and had thereafter committed crimes beyond all reckoning.

'Haven't you added up the score yet, Sir Julius?' Mrs Carstairs said sharply. 'Just look at the time! I should have been in bed long ago.'

'You're not going to bed now,' said Robert thickly. 'Must stay up to see Christmas in.'

'Quite unnecessary,' said Mrs Carstairs firmly. 'I have to get up early tomorrow to go to church, whatever anybody else may intend to do.'

'I fear that that will prove to be impossible,' Dr Bottwink put in. 'From my observation, I should say that the snow will prevent anybody from going to church or anywhere else tomorrow morning.'

Mrs Carstairs looked vexed and alarmed.

'It's no distance to church,' she objected. 'Surely we can have the path cleared as far as that?'

'Who by, my good woman? Who by?' said Robert with an ugly laugh. 'The stable-boys and undergardeners? You seem to forget that there aren't any wage-slaves at Warbeck now. You and Julius have seen to that!'

Mrs Carstairs disregarded him.

'Sir Julius,' she said with dangerous calm, 'would you like me to help you with the scores? You seem to be in some difficulty.'

'No, no, it's quite all right,' Julius mumbled through his cigar, shedding ash upon the table. 'It was a bit difficult, there was so much scoring above the line, but I've got it now. Let me see . . . Eight and six is fourteen and carry one . . . That makes one pound four and fivepence they owe us, Mrs Carstairs. My congratulations!'

'Let me have a look!' Mrs Carstairs reached across the table and seized the score card before Julius could protest. 'I am sure that's wrong! Seven and four's eleven and ten's twenty-one . . . I told you so! It should be one pound four and ninepence! Really, Sir Julius, for a Chancellor of the Exchequer!'

'Well, well,' Sir Julius replied unabashed. 'One doesn't need to be a dab at arithmetic to handle the finances of the State, thank heaven! Why, there was one of my predecessors who didn't even know what decimal points were, and when he saw them for the first time—'

'Yes, yes, Sir Julius,' Mrs Carstairs intervened waspishly. 'I am sure that everyone present has heard that story at least once. And I may say that it has been the stock excuse of inefficient Chancellors ever since.'

'In-eff-icient!' Sir Julius let the syllables fall one by one with an air of shocked amusement. 'Upon my soul, that is about the last epithet I should have ever expected to hear applied to me, from such a source, Mrs Carstairs! That is, I suppose I am correct in assuming that it was intended to apply to me?'

Mrs Carstairs made no direct reply to this challenge. She contented herself with a shrug of the shoulders and a smile that did not seem wholly consistent with the spirit of Christmas.

'Because, if that was the intention,' Sir Julius continued in reproachful tones, 'I think it only proper to point out that that does not appear to be the view of my very loyal collaborator—' His enunciation of the word was not quite so clear as it might have been. He paused, cleared his throat, and repeated defiantly, '– collaborator and colleague, your husband.'

He began ponderously to rise to his feet as though to indicate that the discussion was over; but in vain. Had he been completely sober he would have realised that if one thing could be relied on to provoke a retort it was the mention of Alan Carstairs.

'Yes! My husband *is* loyal!' The devoted wife spoke with breathless speed. Her rather pink and shiny nose was quivering with emotion. 'Too loyal, Sir Julius, some of his best friends think, to consider his own interests! I only hope the interests of the country too do not suffer on account of his disinterestedness. I hope so, I repeat, but there are moments when it becomes a forlorn hope. In my position, my lips are sealed, but since you have chosen to introduce his name into the discussion, let me say quite frankly here and now that I am sure I am not alone in regretting that at such a critical moment in our history the nation's finances should not be in his hands instead of—'

'Instead of those of your humble servant, eh, Mrs Carstairs?' Sir Julius judged that the time had come to pour the oil of his geniality on the waters he had so rashly stirred up. 'Well, well, that is perhaps hardly a subject on which you will expect me to be quite impartial. Perhaps, if you will allow me to say so, it is a subject which is better not discussed – even among friends.' His eyes went round the room and rested for a moment on Dr Bottwink, who was receiving an unexpected sidelight on contemporary English politics. 'But since we are among friends,' he continued, conscious now that he had among his audience

73

someone whom it might conceivably be worth while to impress, 'let me in all sincerity add this: should anything untoward happen to our revered Prime Minister – which Heaven forfend! – and should it in consequence fall to my lot to be charged with the responsibility of forming an administration – as it might, as it might – I do not think that I should need to look for any Chancellor beyond my old friend and companion in arms, Alan Carstairs.'

'Hear, hear, Julius! Hear, hear!' There was a note of tipsy irony in Robert's voice which grated on the Chancellor's sensitive ear.

'Did you say one pound four and ninepence, Mrs Carstairs?' Camilla said quickly. 'I've got it here exactly.' With fingers that trembled slightly she took the money from her bag and passed it across the table.

'Oh, thank you, Camilla dear. That is most honourable of you.'

Robert rose from his seat and lurched over towards his cousin.

'One pound four and ninepence,' he said, a dangerous smile on his full lips. 'Afraid I haven't any cash on me, Julius. It's a commodity that's rather scarce in this branch of the family. Pity, that. You ought to have a bonus for your beautiful speech. Will you take a cheque?'

'Yes, yes, of course, my dear fellow.'

'Splendid! I'll give you one tomorrow, then. Oh, by the way, you don't mind it's being drawn on the account of the League of Liberty and Justice, I suppose?'

Sir Julius started back as if he had been struck. His face had gone suddenly white with anger. Controlling himself with obvious difficulty, he said in a strangled voice, 'If that was meant as a joke, Robert, I can only say that it was in the worst possible taste.'

'No joke at all! I'm perfectly serious. I shouldn't have expected you to be so particular where the cash comes from, so long as you get it. It's not like you, Julius.'

'How dare you suggest that I should take money from such a gang! Let me tell you, young man, your association with this so-called league of yours is putting you in danger – in very grave danger!'

Robert bowed in mock gravity. 'Thanks for the warning, my dear cousin!' he said. 'I can look after myself. At any rate, I don't need a flat-footed copper to give me protection! Where is he, by the way? I don't seem to have noticed him this evening. Is he lurking outside the door with his little notebook and pencil in his hand? Let's have him in! He's just the man we want to make our happy party complete! Perhaps he'll lend me one pound four and ninepence!'

He began to walk towards the door, but Camilla rose quickly and intercepted him.

'Don't be silly, Robert,' she said. 'I'll pay Sir Julius for you, if you like.'

Robert stopped in his stride and looked down on her from his greater height with a crazy leer. 'One pound four and ninepence,' he repeated. 'Do you care for me as much as all that, Camilla? After this afternoon's adventure too? What a beautifully forgiving nature you must have! A pity it should be all wasted, isn't it? But don't stand in my way now. There's the prize boy of Scotland Yard outside, just longing to be let in.'

From opposite ends of the room, Dr Bottwink and Sir Julius converged upon him.

'Lady Camilla, perhaps I—' Dr Bottwink began.

'Robert, you're drunk! You should go to bed at once!' said Sir Julius in the same breath.

Pushing them all on one side, Robert took two strides towards the door. Just as he reached it, it opened from without and Briggs entered. He carried before him a tray on which was a bottle of champagne and half a dozen glasses. Moving with majestic deliberation, he walked across a room that had suddenly fallen quite silent and set his burden down on a side-table.

'What the devil's this for, Briggs?' Robert asked.

'It only wants a few minutes to midnight, Mr Robert,' said Briggs calmly. 'I have brought the champagne to drink in the festive season, according to custom.'

Robert began to laugh, at first with a hoarse chuckle, then more and more loudly, until it seemed as if he could not stop. The mirthless clamour filled the room.

'According to custom!' he crowed. 'That's rich! You're right, Briggs! Let's keep up tradition while we may! The last Christmas in the old home – thanks to Cousin Julius and his pack of robbers! Fill up the glasses, Briggs, and give yourself one too.'

'Very good, sir.' The butler's level tones seemed to belong to a different world from Robert's uncontrolled accents. He opened the bottle and began to fill the glasses.

'Where's the protecting angel, Briggs? He ought to be in on this.'

'The detective-sergeant, sir,' said the butler severely as he continued with his task, 'is refreshing himself in the servants' hall. I think that he will be more at home there. Your glass, my lady.'

76

He handed the tray in turn to Camilla, Mrs Carstairs, Sir Julius and Dr Bottwink. Then he turned to Robert.

'Your glass, Mr Robert,' he said. 'It is almost time.'

'Time marches on!' cried Robert wildly. The wine spilled over the rim of his glass as he lifted it. Then he looked round the room. 'But we've forgotten something, Briggs. The curtains are still drawn and the windows shut. That won't do on Christmas Eve. We've got to let Christmas in!'

'You can't do that, sir,' Briggs protested. 'It's bitter cold outside and snowing hard.'

'What does that matter, man? There's a tradition at stake!' Robert left his glass on the card table and dashed towards the heavy curtains. With two sharp movements he tore them back to their full extent and then flung open the wide french windows. A gust of freezing air blew into the room and a scurry of snowflakes eddied on to the carpet. He stood in the black opening, his hair ruffled by the wind, peering out intently into the night. Then he turned his head and spoke into the room.

'Listen!' he commanded. 'Can't you hear them? Come close to the window, everybody! Closer! Camilla! Briggs! Come on, Julius, a breath of fresh air won't hurt you for once! Can you hear them now?'

As though spellbound, the little group of men and women obeyed his summons and clustered in the piercing cold round the open window. Above the soughing of the wind they could hear the distant chime of church bells.

'Warbeck chimes! Ringing in Christmas, ringing out the Warbecks! Except for fat old Julius, who'll always come out on top whatever happens! Now, listen everybody!' He stepped suddenly back from the window and stood in the middle of the room. Snow plastered the front of his coat, and he was gasping for breath as though he had just finished a race. 'I've got an announcement to make – an important announcement! You mustn't miss it, Camilla. It's – it's—'

He stopped abruptly. The bells had ceased. In their place, the church clock began to sound the quarters.

'Christmas!' he muttered. 'We must have our toast first! Where's my glass? Briggs, you fool, where the hell have you put my glass?'

'It's on the card table, Mr Robert.'

'Ah, here it is!' With an unsteady hand he seized the wine glass as the first stroke of midnight boomed out. 'Are you all ready? Here's to Warbeck Hall, God help the old place!'

He drained the glass, stood for a moment, his face horribly distorted, clutched at his throat with one hand while the glass dropped nervelessly from the other, then pitched heavily forward to lie face downwards on the floor.

'Robert!' Camilla's voice rang out above the last toll of the bell.

'He's fainted!' cried Mrs Carstairs.

'All that drink!' muttered Sir Julius, as he went forward to lift him up.

But Dr Bottwink forestalled him. Kneeling by the recumbent figure, he raised its head and took one quick look at the face before he laid it down again.

'I am afraid he is quite dead,' he said in his quiet, precise voice.

IX

Cyanide

Dr Bottwink's softly spoken words were succeeded by utter silence. For a long moment the little group remained there, voiceless and motionless, the five living as still and quiet as the one dead. Nothing stirred in the room, save for the curtains flapping in the wind from the open window.

Camilla's voice, hoarse and barely recognisable, broke the spell.

'Dead?' she muttered. 'But he can't be dead! It – it isn't possible! He was so alive just now! Robert!' Her voice rose to a wild cry as she ran forward and threw herself on her knees beside the corpse. 'Robert! Listen to me! You must listen! I didn't mean it! I didn't mean—' She broke into a torrent of sobs.

Sir Julius was beside her in a moment and raised her to her feet. She clung to him for support, weeping without restraint, all self-control gone.

'You must try to be brave, my dear girl,' Julius murmured uncertainly. 'Shocking business for us all. I – er – you—' He looked around him, at a loss. 'Mrs Carstairs, don't you think you could get her up to bed? She oughtn't to stay here, and—'

'Of course, of course!' Mrs Carstairs' brisk, practical manner was in refreshing contrast to the Chancellor's helplessness. 'I'll take her upstairs and stay with her as long as necessary. Perhaps you will give me a hand to her room, Briggs? I—'

'A moment!' Dr Bottwink had risen to his feet. 'I do not think that it would be wise for these ladies to leave from here just yet.'

There was an air of quiet authority in his voice that compelled itself upon his hearers. Even Camilla's sobs were hushed. Very deliberately, Dr Bottwink brushed the snow from his knees and then walked over to the window, which he closed, drawing the heavy curtains back into place. In the abrupt silence that fell upon the room as the clamour of the storm was shut out, his carefully spoken words fell on their ears like small pebbles cast one after another into a still pool.

'A sudden death has occurred here,' he said. 'A violent death. It is inevitable – is it not? – that it must be followed by police enquiries. You ladies and gentlemen will be more acquainted than I with the correct procedure laid down by the laws of this country in such matters, but it appears to me that it would be – undesirable, shall I say? – if the witnesses of this tragic occurrence were permitted to disperse before the proper steps are taken. I think that in so suggesting I am speaking in the interests of each one of us.'

'Proper steps?' echoed Sir Julius.

'The proper steps, I apprehend, are to summon the assistance of the police without delay. We have the good fortune to have an officer close at hand.'

'Of course, Sir Julius,' Mrs Carstairs broke in. 'Dr Bottling is quite right. Your man – what's his name? – ought to be told at once. He will know the proper thing to do. Briggs, will you go and find him at once and bring him here? Good Heavens, but this is a dreadful situation!

If my husband were only here, he would know—'

Dr Bottwink interrupted her.

'I think,' he observed, 'that Lady Camilla is about to faint.'

Sir Julius caught her just in time. With Dr Bottwink's assistance he carried her to a sofa, while Briggs went in search of Sergeant Rogers. Mrs Carstairs, whose accomplishments included a training in first aid, attended to her.

'Isn't there any water in the room?' she asked.

'No, but there's still some champagne left in the bottle,' Sir Julius suggested. 'Perhaps a drop of that—'

'Sir Julius!' Dr Bottwink interposed. 'I implore you not to touch that bottle, or anything else on the table.'

The Chancellor of the Exchequer's sense of his own importance had had time to re-establish itself.

'Upon my word, sir,' he said, 'you seem to be taking a good deal upon yourself. What exactly are you suggesting?'

'I am suggesting nothing. But do not the facts speak for themselves?'

'You seem to have jumped to the conclusion that because of what has happened to this unfortunate young man there must have been foul play.'

'I should not call it "play" of any kind,' said Dr Bottwink seriously.

Before any reply could be made, Rogers came running into the room, followed by Briggs. The sergeant's face bore an expression of alarm that gave way to relief at the sight of Sir Julius, and his first words seemed ludicrously inappropriate to the situation.

'Are you all right, sir?' he panted.

'Yes, yes, of course I'm all right,' said Julius testily.

'Why shouldn't I be?'

'I beg your pardon, Sir Julius, but I was told by Mr Briggs I was wanted at once, and I thought—'

His eyes fell on the silent figure stretched on the floor near the window.

'Mr Warbeck!' he exclaimed. 'What has happened?'

'He died,' said Dr Bottwink succinctly, 'after drinking a glass of champagne.'

Stepping carefully across the carpet, Rogers approached the spot where Robert lay.

'You have satisfied yourself that life is extinct, of course, Doctor?' he said.

'I am not a doctor of medicine. But you can judge for yourself.'

'I beg your pardon, sir. In that case—'

He knelt down beside the body for a moment or two. When he rose, he looked grave and at the same time somewhat perplexed. Turning to Sir Julius, he said, 'This is a very unfortunate situation, sir. I am in some difficulty as to the proper procedure.'

Dr Bottwink began to say something, but thought better of it and the sergeant went on, 'This is a matter which should be reported at once to the local police. It is entirely their responsibility. As you know, sir, I am here simply on protection duty. So long as nothing happens to you, I am not concerned, strictly speaking. The investigation of an affair of this nature is entirely outside my sphere.'

'Do you mean that you're going to stand there and do nothing, you ridiculous person?' said Mrs Carstairs.

Sergeant Rogers paid not the least attention to her, but patiently awaited Julius's reply.

'Very well, then, if that is the position, get in touch with the local police at once,' he said.

'I beg your pardon, sir, but that is exactly the trouble. I thought you knew. It is impossible to communicate with the police station or with anybody outside the house. I tried to put through my routine report this evening, and the telephone was dead. The wireless reported at nine o'clock that lines were down all over the country. We are completely cut off.'

'Cut off? But this is absurd! You know as well as I do that I must keep in touch with the Treasury at a time like this, Christmas Day or no Christmas Day. How is the country's business to be carried on, I'd like to know, if I am to be cut off, as you call it?'

'I could not say, sir. But the facts are as I have stated.'

Julius was silent for a moment. Then he said, 'If that is really the case, Rogers, you must do the best you can. You are a police officer, after all.'

'You wish me to undertake this enquiry, sir?'

'Until you can hand it over to the proper authorities – yes.'

'Very good, sir.' Rogers paused as though to collect himself. When he spoke again, his diffidence had vanished. Something almost of a parade-ground rasp had entered into his curt official tones.

'When did death occur?' he asked Sir Julius.

'At twelve o'clock precisely.'

'The clock was striking at the moment,' Mrs Carstairs put in.

'One at a time, please, madam. Was everybody here present when the deceased died?'

'Oh, yes,' Julius assured him. 'Certainly, everybody.

83

That's just—'

'Very good. Now has anything in the room been touched since the death?'

'No, I think not.'

'Yes,' said Mrs Carstairs. 'You shut the window and drew the curtains just now, Dr Bottling.'

'Bottwink,' said the historian automatically. 'Yes, Mrs Carstairs, I did. It was because—'

'Nothing else?' the sergeant pursued.

'No, nothing else.'

'Then I am going to ask you all to leave this room, and not to return to it without my permission. I shall retain the key. I shall require each of you to give me a statement separately, and in the meantime I shall be obliged if you will refrain from discussing the matter among yourselves. You see' – for a moment he became almost human – 'I want your own recollections and not other people's. Will you help me about that?'

'But you're not proposing to take statements from us at this hour of the night, surely?' Julius protested. 'I don't know about anyone else, but I'm in no condition to do anything but sleep after what I've gone through.'

'I am not asking for any consideration for myself,' added Mrs Carstairs pointedly, 'but I should have thought it obvious that there was one person here who should be spared such an ordeal.' She indicated the sofa, where Camilla was lying, still in a dazed stupor.

Sergeant Rogers reflected for a moment. 'I think that I could postpone my questions until the morning,' he said. 'But if I do so, there is one point to be cleared up before anybody leaves.' He turned to Dr Bottwink. 'You said just now that Mr Warbeck died after drinking a glass of champagne. How long after?'

'Immediately. One might say that death came to him in the act of drinking.'

'Apparently as the result of what he drank?'

'Unquestionably. The champagne was poisoned – no doubt with cyanide of potassium.'

'I thought you said you were not a doctor of medicine?'

'Nor am I,' said Dr Bottwink frostily. 'But I have seen such deaths before. One does not easily forget them.'

'Did anybody else drink from the same bottle?'

'All of us, I believe. I certainly did myself.'

'Thank you, sir.' Rogers turned from him and addressed the room at large. 'I am now going to ask each of you to submit to a search.'

'Really, Sergeant!' said Julius. 'Why should this be necessary?'

'For a very plain reason, sir,' said Rogers severely. 'If the deceased was poisoned, and the poison was not in the bottle from which he drank, it follows that it must have been brought into this room by *somebody*.'

'Good God! Do you imagine that I, for example—'

'It is not my business to imagine things, Sir Julius, but you desired me to undertake this enquiry, and I must carry it out in the proper way. Do you mind turning out your pockets, sir?'

'Very well, if you insist,' grumbled the Chancellor. 'Though it seems to me ridiculous to suppose— How do you know that this wretched young man didn't poison himself?' he demanded.

'Naturally, I have that possibility in mind. I shall search

the deceased in due course. Now, sir, if you please.'

The miscellaneous contents of Sir Julius's pockets were emptied out on the card table. They contained nothing more incriminating than a small bottle of white pills, with the name of a well-known London chemist upon the label. The sergeant regarded it suspiciously.

'I think I should detain this for the time being,' he said.

'Heavens, man, don't you know digestive tablets when you see them?'

'No sir. Until an analysis has been made, I don't know what they are. Or whether this bottle has been used to carry anything else.'

'But these are my tablets!' Julius insisted. 'I have to take them every night. I can't possibly do without them.'

'What is your normal dose, sir?'

'Two.'

The detective unscrewed the top of the bottle, shook out two tablets, and gravely handed them across the table. 'That will see you through this evening, at any rate, sir,' he said. 'I'm sure I don't wish to cause you any inconvenience.'

With a grumble, Sir Julius took them and then began stuffing his belongings back into his pockets.

'Now I suppose I may go to bed,' he said.

'Not just yet, please. Perhaps I might deal with the ladies next.'

'You don't mean that you are going to search *me*!' Mrs Carstairs was a figure of outraged virtue.

'No, madam. It will be sufficient if you let me see your handbag. And perhaps you will pass me the other lady's . . . Thank you.'

86

With a practised hand, Rogers eviscerated the two bags given him, without finding anything to interest him. Dr Bottwink and Briggs were then searched in turn, without protest and without result. When he had finished, Julius reiterated his plea to be allowed to go to bed.

'Now that all our characters have been cleared,' he said with a poor attempt at irony, 'I presume that there is no point in keeping us up any longer.'

The sergeant reflected for a moment. 'I am afraid there is still something to be done,' he said. 'But at all events, you will not wish to be kept in here. Mr Briggs, is there another room to which we can go, somewhere fairly warm, if possible?'

Briggs hesitated. 'The warmest place in the house is the housekeeper's room,' he said. 'There is a good fire there and the rest of the staff are in bed. I hardly like to suggest it to these ladies and gentlemen, but—'

'Then for Heaven's sake let's go there and get it over,' said Sir Julius. 'Show me the way, Briggs.' And he made for the door.

It was left to Dr Bottwink to help Mrs Carstairs to raise Camilla to her feet.

'Do you think that you can manage to walk, my lady?' he said gently.

'Yes, thank you,' she murmured, and with his support began to walk towards the door. Half-way across the room, she stopped and looked back at the silent figure by the window. 'We're – we're not going to leave him there – like that?' she murmured pitifully.

'I am sorry, my lady, but it is necessary,' said Rogers firmly. 'I trust it will not be for long.'

He remained behind a minute or two after the others. Before leaving he satisfied himself that all the windows were secure. Then he turned out the lights and locked the door behind him, pocketing the key.

The housekeeper's room was small and square and snug. By the time that Rogers reached it the dejected little party from the drawing-room had settled themselves in its shabby but comfortable chairs round a glowing coal fire. Briggs, unasked, had put a kettle on the hob and was busying himself preparing tea. Compared with what Rogers had just left, it was a cosy, almost domestic scene.

'I have examined the clothing of the deceased,' he said abruptly. 'So far as I am able to tell at present, there are no traces of poison upon his person.'

'That is to be expected, is it not?' said Dr Bottwink diffidently. 'A lethal dose of this poison is, after all, a very small object. One would not think to find any surplus left over in the pockets.'

'That is so,' the detective agreed. 'What I am looking for is anything that could have served as a container. So far, I have failed to find it.'

'What I fail to understand,' complained Julius, with a huge yawn, 'is why you should make this an excuse for keeping us all out of our beds.'

'Sir Julius,' said Rogers firmly, 'I must ask you, please, to try to appreciate the position. Barring accident, which seems most improbable, this is a case either of suicide or of murder.' It was the first time that the word which had been in the back of the minds of everyone present had been used. The sound of it, spoken though it was in a flat, conversational tone, sent an uneasy stir round the room. 'For the time being, I am compelled to act upon the assumption that it is a case of murder. If it is, it was obviously committed by one of you people here now.' He paused for a moment, and as he did so, his hearers, crowded together in the tiny room, seemed to shrink into themselves, so as to shift apart from one another, as though each was oppressed with a sudden desire to lose contact with his neighbour. 'In the circumstances,' Rogers went on dryly, 'there is one obvious enquiry which I must make. I am single-handed, which means that it will take longer than it would in the ordinary way.'

'I follow,' said Dr Bottwink. 'Before we retire to rest, you wish to search our bedrooms to see if any of us has a supply of cyanide concealed in his wardrobe.'

'Precisely.'

'You seem to know all about it, Dr Bottling,' observed Mrs Carstairs acidly.

'Bottwink. Yes, I have the advantage of having been the subject of police perquisitions before now.'

'May I,' said Camilla faintly, 'may I be the first to go to bed, please?'

'If you wish it, my lady. I should prefer to conduct the search in your presence, and you will probably wish the other lady to be present also. We can go now. Will the others please remain here until I return?'

'The tea is just ready, if your ladyship would like a cup before you go,' said Briggs.

'Thank you, Briggs, I should like it.'

In the act of pouring out the tea, Briggs gave a sudden start. He put the pot down on the table with a little crash and turned to the detective.

'Is it cyanide of potassium you're looking for, Mr Rogers?' he said.

'Yes.'

'I've only just remembered. I have some in my pantry.'

'What?'

'I got it for taking wasps' nests last summer, and it's been there ever since. Would you like to see it?'

'You had better show it to me right away.'

'Very good, Mr Rogers. Your tea, my lady. Perhaps you ladies and gentlemen won't mind helping yourselves. This way, Mr Rogers.'

'There it is,' said Briggs. 'In that little cupboard next the sink. Perhaps you'd like to look yourself. It's not locked.'

The sergeant walked across to the cupboard indicated and opened it.

'When did you go to this cupboard last?' he asked.

'I really couldn't say for sure, Mr Rogers. It isn't often I go there – it's just got a few odds and ends in it one doesn't often want. Wait a minute, though . . . I remember now, a week or two ago Dr Bottwink was showing me a bit of old panelling he'd found at the back of it. He was very interested in it, though it's nothing to look at. Can you see the panelling, Mr Rogers?'

'Yes,' said Rogers. 'I can see the panelling.'

He closed the cupboard and turned an expressionless face in the direction of Briggs.

'I suppose it was marked "Poison"?' he said.

'Yes, that's right. A little blue bottle, with "Poison" on the label in big letters. It – Mr Rogers, do you mean it's gone?'

Rogers nodded. 'We'd better be getting back to the

housekeeper's room,' he said. 'At any rate, we know now what to look for.'

On the way, he turned to the butler and asked him one more question.

'How many rooms are there in this house?'

'I've never counted them, Mr Rogers, but the guide-books say fifty-three.'

'Fifty-three,' he repeated. 'And it may be in any one of them — if it's in the house at all, by now.' He sighed. 'I think I've heard you complain that you are short-handed, Mr Briggs!'

More than an hour later, red-eyed but still untiring, Rogers was completing his examination of the butler's bedroom. Briggs was the last to go to bed. One by one, all the guests had been escorted to their rooms and had watched while a pitiless but fruitless search had been made through their effects.

'That finishes it,' he said at last. 'I'm sorry to have made such a mess of your things, Mr Briggs. You'll be glad of some rest now.'

'So will you, Mr Rogers, I reckon. It's turned two already.'

The sergeant shook his head. 'I've still some work to do,' he said. 'This job is like a sailor's. You've got to know how to go without sleep when necessary. Good night! I'll be seeing you in the morning. Better not say anything about what's happened to the staff until I've spoken to them.'

'Very good, Mr Rogers. Good night! I—' A sudden thought struck him, and his face changed. 'His lordship!' he murmured. 'Who's going to break this to his lordship?'

X

Dr Bottwink at Breakfast

Dr Bottwink was the first to put in an appearance at breakfast-time on Christmas morning. He stumped briskly into the dining-room on his short legs, his round sallow cheeks perhaps a shade paler than usual, but otherwise showing little sign of being affected by the experiences of the night before. He bent down over the small fire that was smouldering mournfully in the grate in an endeavour to warm his hands, and then, after a reproachful glance at the clock, turned to stare out of the window. It was a profitless occupation. His view was limited to a few yards of snow-covered lawn. Beyond that, everything was shrouded in a dense fog. The air was very still. Nothing stirred except a few starlings, their feathers puffed out against the bitter cold, which were moving about on the snow with an air of utter dejection. Dr Bottwink had plenty of time to enjoy this prospect before Briggs entered with a tray.

'Good morning, Briggs!'

'Good morning, sir.'

'It would scarcely be in order, I apprehend, if I were to wish you a merry Christmas?'

'Under the circumstances, sir, I think not,' said Briggs severely, as he set down the breakfast things on the sideboard. 'Though I am grateful for the intention, all the same,' he added.

'I have spent Christmas in many countries,' Dr Bottwink observed, 'and in very different conditions, but never quite such a strange one as this. It is odd, too, that this is the first time that I have actually been snowed up. And now this fog! The English climate is certainly unpredictable. I take it that we are still cut off from the outside world?'

'Yes, sir.'

Dr Bottwink went to the sideboard and took up the two silver jugs as though to pour himself a cup of coffee. Then he put them down and instead contented himself with lifting the lids and inspecting their contents.

'And yet this milk appears to be fresh enough, Briggs,' he said. 'How is that?'

'A man managed to get through from the home farm an hour ago, sir. I asked him whether he thought it would be feasible to make his way to the village during the day and he was very doubtful. We are in a hollow here and the snow has drifted many feet deep.'

Dr Bottwink sighed. 'It is a thousand pities I did not think to bring a pair of skis,' he said, 'though I could scarcely have found my way in conditions like this, in any case. How long will this go on, I wonder?'

'Not very long, I hope, sir. This morning's wireless gives some prospect of a thaw setting in. A day or two should see the end of it.'

'A day or two! That can be a very long time in certain situations.'

'Quite so, sir.'

'Perhaps you are asking yourself the same question as I am?'

'Pardon, sir?'

'The question that is exercising my mind is whether we shall, all of us, live to see the end of it.'

'*Sir?*'

'Don't look so shocked, Briggs. One must be realistic in matters of this sort. If somebody is at large in this house with a supply of poison, there is no reason that I can see why that individual should not choose to employ it again. The conditions are, after all, ideal.'

The butler made no reply. He appeared to be absorbed in contemplation of the breakfast table. Very deliberately he straightened a fork which seemed already to be in perfect alignment with its neighbour and then said in a low, hurried tone, 'Will you be requiring me any more, sir?'

'I? Not at all, Briggs. Though one is naturally glad of company at such a time, do you not find it so? But I must not keep you from your duties. You will have observed that I have not yet begun my breakfast. I shall wait for some other guest to arrive before I do so. Should anything untoward occur it would be as well to have witnesses.'

'I don't know what you mean, sir, I'm sure.'

'I mean simply this, Briggs – that the life that it has been my misfortune to lead has made me temperamentally suspicious. Obviously, you are not of a suspicious nature, or you would not be in such a hurry to go.'

'I don't understand you, sir.'

'You astonish me. Well, if I must put it bluntly – let us suppose that somebody – Sir Julius, shall we say – for the purposes of illustration merely, of course – were to die from cyanide poison after drinking this excellent coffee, it would be unfortunate for us both – for you that you prepared it, and equally so for me that I was left unattended here long enough to insert a lethal dose. Each would find himself in the disagreeable situation of having to defend himself by accusing the other. However, it may not come to that, and I am prepared to take that risk, if you are.'

Deeply troubled, Briggs hesitated for a time, and then said, 'I will stay until somebody comes down, sir.'

'I think you are wise, Briggs. Since to your knowledge there is at present nothing in the least unhealthy in our breakfast, you are assuring the continued existence of the house-party for one meal, at any rate. I hope one of them will be down soon. I am beginning to feel decidedly peckish.' He smiled his appreciation of his own command of English slang and took a turn up and down the room. 'You would not care to join me in a cup of coffee, Briggs? That would at least serve to pass the time, and we should be, so to speak, keeping an eye on each other.'

'Thank you, sir, I breakfasted an hour ago.'

'No doubt, but another cup would do you no harm, I am sure.'

The butler shook his head. 'It would be hardly suitable, sir,' he said.

'I follow. A butler should not partake of even so much as a cup of coffee in the presence of a guest – not even when the house is cut off from the world by snow, not even on the morrow of a murder. I apologise for suggesting anything so dishonourable. We will await the others, then. By the way, I suppose there will be only two of them? Lady Camilla will no doubt be remaining in bed.'

'No, sir. Her ladyship has decided to get up, the maid informs me.'

'Indeed? That young woman has courage – and more

strength than would appear upon the surface. And Lord Warbeck? I should have asked after him before. Is he to be up or down today?'

'His lordship is breakfasting in bed, sir. I do not think that it is his intention to get up today.'

'That I can well understand. But at least he is breakfasting. That shows a truly admirable phlegm. He is not, then, completely prostrated by the news?'

'He – he knows nothing about it as yet, sir. I did not mention the – the – the happening of last night.'

'Really, Briggs, if I may so express myself, your self-effacement appears to me to be more than human. But I suppose you would merely tell me that it is improper for an English butler to mention a matter of life and death to his employer.'

'It is not like that at all, sir,' Briggs replied, with a rare trace of warmth in his voice. 'If there's anyone in the world who's got the right to speak to his lordship about such a thing, I reckon that I have. It was just that when it came to the point – when I saw his lordship lying there, tired and weak but contented in a way, and glad to see me with the breakfast tray – well, I hadn't the courage, and that's the fact.'

If Dr Bottwink was moved by the butler's evident distress, he did not show it. 'So!' he said, in a surprised tone. 'And yet, Briggs, I should not have taken you for a coward. Then I suppose his lordship wished you a happy Christmas, just as I proposed to do just now, and you had to respond and wish him the same?'

Briggs, nodded, speechless.

'That must have been a difficult moment for you. But

all the same, we must face the fact that he has to be told some time. He will no doubt be expecting his son to come and see him during the morning.'

'Yes, sir,' said Briggs huskily. 'He did in fact instruct me to ask all the party to see him as soon as they had breakfasted in order to wish them' – his voice faltered – 'the compliments of the season, sir.'

The historian sighed. 'In that case, it looks as though this news will have to be broken by what the English Parliament so illogically calls a Committee of the whole House,' he said. 'Well, there is safety in numbers, at least.'

As if to add point to his remark, Sir Julius came into the room at this moment. There were heavy pouches under his eyes and he had cut his chin in shaving.

'Good morning, Sir Julius,' said Dr Bottwink politely.

'Morning. Morning, Briggs. What have you got for us for breakfast?'

'Scrambled eggs and kipper, Sir Julius. There is some cereal, if you wish it.'

'Can't stand the stuff. All right, Briggs, you needn't wait. I'll help myself.'

'Very good, Sir Julius.'

Whatever suspicions anybody else might have about the food provided at Warbeck Hall, the Chancellor of the Exchequer evidently had none. He helped himself largely from the sideboard and carried his plate over to the table, where he seated himself with his back to the window and fell to. Dr Bottwink, with a sigh of relief followed his example, taking a chair opposite to him.

The historian was too well versed in the customs of the English to be surprised at the fact that his companion preferred to breakfast without acknowledging by word or sign that he was not alone. Nevertheless, as the meal proceeded, the silence became more than usually oppressive. He occupied himself by speculating on the reasons that made this meal more funereal than all the other dumb breakfasts that he had eaten in the past. Was it, he wondered, the fact that there were no newspapers to act as a defensive screen against one's neighbour? Or the uncanny stillness of the blank world outside? Or was he affected by the reaction from the events of the night before, the consciousness that beyond that door, a few yards away, lay the body of a murdered man? Whatever the answer, it would be interesting to know whether, beneath his apparent concentration on his food, Sir Julius also was conscious of the strain.

Eventually, Julius gave him his answer. Just when it seemed that the silence was to remain unbroken for all time, he paused in the act of buttering a piece of toast, looked very hard across the table, cleared his throat and said in an accusing tone:

'Dr Bottwink, you are a foreigner.'

'I am bound to admit that that is so,' the historian replied with complete gravity.

'Naturally, you are not altogether familiar with our customs, our habits, our way of life.'

'Very true. Indeed, I may say that although I have lived in this country for several years, and have even ventured to write a book or two upon it, I continue to be astonished at my ignorance of the three subjects you mention. I presume that they are three distinct subjects?' he added. 'My knowledge is so hazy that left to myself I should have regarded them as synonymous.'

Julius frowned. This pertinacious alien was trying to be altogether too clever.

'That,' he said severely, 'is not the point. What I want to make clear is this: the – er – the unfortunate occurrence that we witnessed last night was not in any way typical of our English way of life. In fact, I think it would be fairly described as entirely un-English. It is particularly painful to me to think that any foreigner should have been present at such a moment. The last thing in the world that I should desire would be for you to imagine that this shocking business was anything but quite exceptional.'

'Indeed, yes,' Dr Bottwink murmured. 'Even the weather, Briggs assures me, is phenomenal.'

'I am *not* discussing the weather, sir,' Julius barked.

'I apologise. My comment was unwarrantably frivolous. May I say at once that I appreciate very much your solicitude on my behalf. I can assure you that I fully understand that what I was unlucky enough to experience last night was not at all what would normally be expected in an English household – particularly,' he added with a little bow, 'at a time when this country is in the full enjoyment of so progressive a government.'

'I don't see that the government of which I have the honour to be a member has anything to do with it,' Julius grumbled.

'Exactly! That is, of course, my point. In less favoured countries anything of this nature might be expected to have a political flavour – political repercussions, even. But perhaps I should not have said that. Your own position, Sir Julius, must, of course, be to some extent affected by the death of the heir to your cousin.'

Sir Julius had gone rather red. 'I prefer not to discuss that,' he said.

'Naturally. Although, of course, it is unfortunately the kind of topic which can hardly avoid discussion sooner or later. I was only going on to say that from a purely selfish point of view – if I might venture hypothetically to attribute selfishness to you – you may come to regard it as not altogether unfortunate that an obscure alien was among the assistants at this tragedy.'

By this time Julius had obviously begun to regret that he had ever ventured to embark upon a breakfast table conversation with Dr Bottwink. Once let this fellow start talking, there was no stopping him. He talked like a book too, not like a human being. It was more than one could stand at that hour of the day. But it was not only his conversational style that was objectionable; the matter of it, to Sir Julius's thinking, was becoming definitely unpleasant.

'I don't know what you're talking about,' he muttered, in a tone that was clearly intended to put an end to the discussion. But Dr Bottwink seemed incapable of taking a hint.

'No?' he said. 'You must forgive me if I fail to make myself clear. It is perhaps a tribute to your British instinct for fair play that what came immediately to my mind did not also occur to yours. You see,' – he adjusted his spectacles with a gesture that somehow invested the room with the atmosphere of a lecture hall – 'as the good Sergeant Rogers so crudely but forcibly puts it, this young man has in all human probability been murdered. That being so, the suspects are, conveniently from his point of view, but lamentably from ours, extremely few. He has to choose between a Cabinet Minister, a young lady of the aristocracy, the wife of a rising politician, a trusted family servant and a foreign savant of mixed parentage and doubtful nationality. To effect the arrest of any one of the first three I have enumerated would clearly provoke a scandal of the first magnitude. To nab – I believe that is the word? – to *nab* a family butler would shake the faith of the British public in one of their most cherished institutions. How fortunate, then, that there should be ready to hand a scapegoat for whom nobody in England can possibly care a brass farthing!'

'You are talking nonsense, sir,' said Sir Julius thickly, 'and pernicious nonsense at that! I make all due allowance, I hope, for the position in which you find yourself, but as a former Home Secretary I resent very deeply the suggestion that the police in this country allow themselves to be influenced in any way by – by such influences as you suggest. Or any influences,' he added defiantly.

He pushed his coffee cup away from him with a gesture of disgust and rose from the table. Dr Bottwink remained seated.

Taking no notice of the Chancellor's outburst, he went on meditatively:

'Of course, it may not come to an arrest. Perhaps the good Rogers will find himself unable to fix the blame upon any one individual among us five. We shall all of us then remain to some extent under a cloud for the rest of our lives. In that case, you will admit, Sir Julius, that in your peculiarly vulnerable position, particularly when in due course you will have succeeded to the title of Lord Warbeck, it will be an advantage to you to be able to silence whisperers by pointing to such an obviously disreputable and suspicious character as myself. No Englishman, not even your warmest political opponent, asked to choose between us two as potential criminals, would hesitate to say—'

But Julius had had enough.

'I can't listen to any more of this rubbish!' he said, and made for the door.

He was out of luck. Just when he was within a few feet of escape from his tormentor, the door opened in his face and he found himself confronted by Mrs Carstairs. Politeness compelled him to stand aside and wish her good morning, and before he could resume his march to freedom he was caught up and swept back into the room again.

'Oh, Sir Julius, I *am* so glad you are still here!' she said. 'You have finished breakfast, I see, but you will stay and give me a little moral support while I drink a cup of coffee, won't you? Goodness knows, I don't feel capable of eating anything on a morning like this! . . . No, don't bother, I can help myself . . . Oh, thank you, Dr Bottling, that is kind of you . . . Yes, two lumps, please. What is under that cover? . . . Oh, well, perhaps a small kipper, if you don't mind. After all, as I always tell my husband, one must keep one's strength up. If only *he* were here, he would know what to do. One feels so defenceless and alone . . . Yes, Sir Julius, do smoke, it won't disturb me a bit . . . Oh, don't go, Dr Bottling . . . What? . . . I beg your pardon, I am always so stupid at names. Don't go, I feel that at a moment like this we all want to stick together, don't you?'

'There is a great deal of truth in what you say, Mrs

Carstairs,' said Dr Bottwink gravely, as he passed her the toast.

'I have passed such a *wretched* night,' Mrs Carstairs went on, as she attacked her kipper with gusto. 'All night I have been tossing and turning, racking my brains to think of what could have possessed that poor young man to kill himself. Can it have been on account of some woman, do you suppose? And yet when one thinks of Camilla, obviously head over heels in love with him—'

'You think that Robert committed suicide?' put in Julius, a shade eagerly.

'But he must have, Sir Julius, must he not? After all, we were all there. We saw him.'

'We saw him die, madame,' said Dr Bottwink sombrely.

'That is the same thing, isn't it? I mean, any other suggestion would be too shocking!'

'Because a suggestion is shocking it is not necessarily untrue, Mrs Carstairs.'

'Dr Bottwink,' said Julius acidly, 'prefers to believe that Robert was the victim of a hideous crime.'

'Indeed, no, Sir Julius! There is no preference in the matter. I have not excluded any possibility, I can assure you. Merely, I judge to the best of my powers from the evidence, as will do, I doubt not, Sergeant Rogers.'

'Don't talk to me about Sergeant Rogers!' cried Mrs Carstairs. 'That man is a fool, if ever I saw one. The mess he made in my bedroom last night with his ridiculous search was quite unbelievable! But seriously, Dr Bottwink, you can't possibly think that one of us could have—' She left the sentence unfinished.

'When I am told that I cannot possibly think anything,

my nature is so contradictory that I immediately begin to think about it. Have you not found that in your own experience?'

'Certainly not!'

'That is very interesting from the psychological standpoint. Perhaps the faculty of imposing control upon the thoughts is the secret of English party politics. What do you think, Sir Julius?'

Julius ground his cigarette end into his saucer, rose to his feet and stared out of the window for a moment before replying.

'I think,' he said finally, 'that there is a great deal in what Mrs Carstairs says.'

'Oh, thank you, Sir Julius. I knew that you would agree with me. It is such a comfort to know, at a time like this—'

Julius interrupted her without ceremony. 'Quite clearly,' he went on, slowly and loudly, 'this was a case of suicide. Any other suggestion is simply not to be entertained.'

'But—' said Dr Bottwink.

'After all,' Julius proceeded in a louder voice than ever, 'as Mrs Carstairs has pointed out, we were there. We saw what happened.'

'Precisely,' said Dr Bottwink, 'and it is because of what I saw—'

'*We saw what happened,*' Julius repeated, more emphatically than ever. 'Apart from Lady Camilla and Briggs, we are the sole witnesses. I propose to have a talk to Briggs in due course. He was probably not in a position to see very much, in any event. Mrs Carstairs, no doubt you will have an opportunity to discuss matters with Lady Camilla. Nobody else will be in a position to contradict what we say.' He looked very hard at Dr Bottwink and went on, 'I can only speak for myself, of course, but I may say that I have a distinct recollection of seeing my cousin place something – what it was I can only guess, of course – in his glass immediately before he drank from it.'

'How very odd that you should say that, Sir Julius!' Mrs Carstairs put in quickly. 'Because I was just going to say exactly the same thing myself. I should have mentioned it at the time, only, of course, we were all so upset, but I can remember now seeing – er – well, seeing exactly what you said just now. I shall make a point of telling Sergeant Rogers.'

Sitting very upright in his chair, Dr Bottwink looked from Mrs Carstairs to Sir Julius and back again. His face was quite expressionless and he allowed an appreciable time to elapse before he spoke.

'I see,' he said. There was another long, uncomfortable pause. 'I see,' he repeated. 'I regret, Sir Julius, that I am a very bad hand at lying.'

'Really!' Julius was all righteous indignation. 'That is not a word that I—'

'No.' The historian's voice had taken on a cutting edge. 'It is a most un-British word, is it not? I should have said – but what does it signify what pretty euphemisms I use or do not use? You wish to hush this thing up – that is all that it amounts to. Well, I shall not stand in your way, though I cannot promise to assist. After all, this is no affair of mine. I have not been taught the English way of life. You may put wool on the eyes of Sergeant Rogers, if you can. Only I should warn you that you will not find him al-together so stupid as you think.'

So saying, he got up and marched out of the room without further ceremony.

After he had gone, there was a moment's embarrassed silence. Then Mrs Carstairs, without looking at Sir Julius, murmured, 'Do you think he will – er – be all right?'

'I think so,' Julius assured her. 'He's a thoroughly tiresome fellow, but he will see reason. As he says, it's no affair of his. He has no interest in making mischief.'

'I hope you are right, Sir Julius. I must say I didn't like his attitude at all.'

'You didn't get the worst of it, I can tell you. Do you know, before you came down the fellow was practically hinting that I had killed Robert for the sake of inheriting the peerage! I ask you, me!' He laughed mirthlessly.

'Ridiculous, Sir Julius! In your position too!' Mrs Carstairs joined in the laugh. 'But still – it just shows the sort of thing ignorant people will say. That is why it is so important—'

'Exactly. Now I don't think Briggs will give any trouble at all. You can leave him to me. So far as Camilla is concerned—'

'Camilla darling!' Mrs Carstairs rose to her feet as the door opened. 'We were just speaking of you! How brave of you to come downstairs. I thought you would be spending the day in bed.'

'There's not much point in staying in bed if you can't sleep,' said Camilla in a hard, flat voice. 'No, thank you, Sir Julius. I can help myself. I only want a piece of toast and something to drink.'

She sat down at the table, her back rigid, her face a cold,

white mask. At a sign from Mrs Carstairs, Julius got up and left the two women alone.

'Camilla,' began Mrs Carstairs gently, 'Sir Julius and I were saying when you came in—'

'Saying something about me – I know. You've mentioned that already. Shall I tell you what it was? You were saying that Robert had treated me like a cad, and that if anybody had a reason for killing him I had.'

'No, no, Camilla! Nothing of the sort, I promise you.'

'Well, it's the truth, isn't it? I'll tell you something else which perhaps you don't know. Up to two minutes to midnight last night I was wishing him dead, and now I just wish I was dead myself. Silly, isn't it?'

'Camilla dear, you must not say things like that! Can't you see how dangerous that sort of talk can be?'

'Dangerous?' Camilla echoed with a bitter smile.

'If you were to say a thing like that to that sergeant person, Heaven knows what he might think.'

'I expect he's ready to think the worst of all of us, anyway. I'm past caring.'

'But you *must* care, Camilla, for all our sakes. Now, Sir Julius and I have been talking this whole thing over and we feel that there's a danger of a terrible mistake being made. If you can only help us to see that the *real* truth about this dreadful affair is known—'

Her voice flowed on, earnest and persuasive, and it was quite difficult to tell from her face whether Camilla was listening or not.

XI

John Wilkes and William Pitt

The muniment room was darker than ever that morning, by reason of the snow that had piled itself thickly against its narrow windows, and it was, if anything, even colder than it had been the day before; but Dr Bottwink entered it with a sigh of relief. He had gone there immediately on leaving the breakfast table, partly out of habit, but partly, as he realised when he looked around him, in response to an instinct that drove him to seek refuge from the horrors and perplexities of the present in the only world that was entirely real to him.

He closed the door behind him with a sigh of relief. Nothing, he was quick to reassure himself, had been touched. Sergeant Rogers had evidently not yet extended his search to this remote corner of the house. His papers remained precisely as he had left them. On the desk still lay the half-illegible document that he had abandoned un-deciphered when Briggs had summoned him to meet the house-party at tea-time yesterday. Dr Bottwink smiled bitterly to himself as he confirmed the fact. Yesterday! Could it be as recent as that? He shrugged his shoulders. Yesterday was history already, and ugly, sordid history at that. It was no more real and no less remote than the date when the tiresome little manuscript yonder had come into existence. Perhaps some future historian might find yesterday worth investigating and recording, but he doubted it. Sergeant Rogers might write its history, if he could; he – Bottwink – preferred the eighteenth century.

He looked at his watch. In less than half an hour's time he was due to join the others in Lord Warbeck's room to perform the grisly ceremony of wishing him the compliments of the season. Much though he would have wished to do so, it was a duty he could hardly refuse. There was no time, then, to do any serious work. All the same, since he was there, he might as well glance again at the document. He could, perhaps, read enough to assure himself that it was of no importance. It was worth trying. He would give it a quarter of an hour, or twenty minutes at the most . . . He settled himself at the desk, switched on the reading lamp, carefully polished his glasses and drew the yellowed sheet towards him.

Familiar as he was with the atrocious script of the third Lord Warbeck, he was for some time completely unable to make head or tail of the blotted scrawl. He would have abandoned the task altogether, had not some sixth sense told him that it was worth while to persist. At last, first a name and then a date emerged from the welter of ink marks. The name was one familiar enough to every student of history, but Dr Bottwink had never encountered it before in the Warbeck papers. In conjunction with that particular date, it was possible – likely, even – that it might prove to be the clue to something important. With a growing sense of excitement, he bent himself afresh to his task. Fortified with a magnifying glass and other specimens of Lord Warbeck's handwriting, he made steady progress. Little by little the whole faded document came alive and made sense. Finally he mastered it, down to the last letter. He read and re-read it with anxious care, and then, taking out his pen, set himself laboriously to transcribe it.

Sitting there at his desk in that freezing atmosphere, Dr Bottwink felt the warm glow of triumph steal through his veins.

Here was reality – here was truth! Here in his hand was the record of the third Lord Warbeck's conversation with John Wilkes at the height of the great Middlesex election campaign, set down on the very day that it had taken place. The fretful dreams of the twentieth century faded away and there was left only Dr Wenceslaus Bottwink with a historical discovery that was destined to confound all the experts – to the number of at least half a dozen – who were capable of understanding its significance. It was a solemn and a joyful moment, such as comes to a man only once or twice in a lifetime.

'My word, sir, but you are pretty cold in here!'

The historian looked up. Through the thick lenses of his reading glasses he could make out the blurred form of a large man standing by the door at the other end of the room. Removing his glasses, he was able to see him more clearly. Slowly and with a painful effort he emerged from the pulsating actuality of the Middlesex election of 1768 and confronted this grey shadow of the present.

'Ah! Sergeant Rogers!' he said, rising stiffly from his chair. 'Good morning!'

'I wonder whether I could have a word or two with you, sir.'

'Of course, of course, I am entirely at your service. Only

– I have just remembered, I have an appointment to see Lord Warbeck this morning. Perhaps I should go to him first.'

The detective looked at him oddly.

'I don't think his lordship will be wanting to see anybody just at present,' he said in a sombre tone. 'Have you been up here all the morning?' he went on.

'All the morning?' Dr Bottwink pulled his old-fashioned silver watch from his pocket. 'But it is impossible! I seem to have been here for more than two hours!'

'That leaves us just time enough for our little chat before lunch,' returned Rogers equably.

'By all means, Sergeant. I repeat, I am at your service. Two hours! I had simply not noticed the passage of time. But will you not seat yourself? Let me clear these books from the chair for you.'

'No,' said Rogers very firmly. 'No thank you, all the same. I don't know how it is with you, sir, but I prefer to do my work in the warm when I can. I came to ask whether you would mind stepping down to the library for a moment or two.'

'Certainly – or should the affirmative reply to that question be certainly not? At all events, I will come with you immediately. Now that you mention it, this room is on the cold side.'

'That was another little thing you had not noticed, perhaps, sir?' said Rogers with a faintly malicious smile, standing aside to let Dr Bottwink pass.

'I had other things to think about than the temperature,' he replied. He paused in the doorway and looked back at the desk, where lay side by side the dingy old memorandum and the clean new transcript he had made of it. With a regretful sigh, he bade farewell to the age of reason and preceded the sergeant down the narrow stone stairway.

'So you don't notice things very much, Dr Bottwink?' said Rogers, as he settled himself in an armchair in front of the library fire.

'Pardon?'

'The time of day – whether it is hot or cold – things like that – you don't notice them?'

'Ah, I comprehend you! The absent-minded professor, that favourite figure of British humour – is that the rôle you cast me for, Sergeant? Well, it is true enough in a way, I suppose. But only in a certain way, you must understand. When one is absorbed in an undertaking of real importance, one does not notice trivialities – that is understandable enough, is it not? But in matters of ordinary life, I flatter myself that I know a hawk from a handsaw.'

'A hawk from a – what was that you said?'

'No matter – the phrase is not original. I thought it would be familiar to you. In plain, police English, I can tell a live man from a dead, and a natural death from a violent one, particularly when it takes place before my eyes. I suppose I am right in assuming, Sergeant, that that is the subject you wished to discuss with me?'

Rogers did not reply. His heavy face was devoid of all expression save fatigue and he was gazing into the fire through half-closed eyes. Suddenly he turned towards Bottwink and shot out an abrupt question.

'Just what sort of a professor are you, Dr Bottwink?'

Patiently the historian enumerated his degrees and qualifications.

'You have got around quite a bit, haven't you?'

Dr Bottwink's lips twisted into a wintry smile.

'Perhaps it would be more accurate to say that I had been pushed around,' he observed gently.

'What exactly were your political affiliations in Czechoslovakia?'

'I was to the left, of course.'

'Of course?'

'I mean that my – my leftism, shall we call it, was the natural cause of my being pushed around.'

'H'm. Then you were in Vienna for some time, I gather?'

'Yes. I was invited to deliver a course of lectures there. The course remains uncompleted.'

'That was during the Dolfuss regime?'

'Yes. Let me anticipate your next question by observing that I was anti-Dolfuss. That is why the lectures were interrupted, naturally. I am anti-clerical, anti-Fascist – in short, you may write me down as one of nature's Antis.'

'Would a shorter way of describing you be to say that you are a communist, Dr Bottwink?'

The historian shook his head.

'Alas!' he said. 'Once, perhaps, it might have been so, but now I am only too conscious that were I in Moscow I should find myself in the uncomfortable position of being anti-Stalin. If I had to define my attitude today, I should say – but why should I waste your time, Sergeant? There are only two things you wish to know about me, and I will relate them to you. One: I am, as strongly as any man could be, opposed to the League of Liberty and Justice. Two: I did not, for that or any other reason, kill the Honourable Mr Robert Warbeck.'

Whether Rogers was impressed or not by Bottwink's words it was impossible to say. He vouchsafed no reply of any kind. Instead, he fumbled in his pockets, produced from one a two-ounce tin of tobacco, from the other a packet of cigarette papers, and proceeded to roll himself a cigarette. When he had lighted it he began again on a wholly different subject.

'This bottle of poison in the pantry cupboard,' he said. 'Describe it to me. What did it look like?'

'I have not the least idea.'

'Are you telling me that it wasn't there?'

'I have no reason to doubt that it was there. Merely I did not observe it.'

'You went at least twice to this cupboard, I understand. Once when you examined this old bit of woodwork—'

'Linen-fold panelling.'

'— and again when you showed it to Briggs. Do you mean to say that on neither occasion you noticed what must have been right under your nose?'

'I was interested in the cupboard – or, to be more accurate, in the back of the cupboard – and not in its contents. I am a historian, Sergeant, and not a poisoner. *Chacun à son métier.*'

'And you did not go back to the cupboard a third time?'

'Certainly not. I had no occasion to do so. Its interest was exhausted for me.'

'Your interest in the cupboard, or in the poison?'

'I repeat, I did not observe any poison there.'

'Your powers of observation seem to be very selective, Dr Bottwink.'

'That is so. You put the position, if I may say so, with admirable clarity.'

'Then I suppose you will tell me that your observation of what took place last night is of no value, and I should be wasting my time if I were to ask you any questions about it.'

'On the contrary. I was keenly interested in everything that occurred. I think that my observation is as good as that of – of anybody else.'

'I should like to test that. Did you observe Mr Warbeck put anything into his glass before he drank?'

'I did not observe it,' said Dr Bottwink, emphatically.

'Yet Sir Julius, Mrs Carstairs and Briggs are all equally confident that he did. How do you account for that, sir?'

Dr Bottwink was silent.

'Well? What do you say?'

'If they all agree,' he said slowly, 'if they all agree, who am I to disagree? But do they agree? That is the question I ask myself.'

'I have just told you that they do.'

'Pardon me, Sergeant, but you have told me no such thing. You have said that they are all equally confident of a fact. You do not mention the Lady Camilla, which is perhaps significant. But further, you have not said that they agree as to the moment at which and the circumstances in which this fact is said to have occurred. That is the test, is it not? I may be anti-clerical, but at least I have read my Bible.'

'And what has the Bible to do with it, may I ask?'

'I was referring to the story of Susanna and the Elders, with which an officer of your experience must be very familiar.'

'I am,' said Rogers shortly.

He remained silent for a time. Dr Bottwink, with the air of a debater who has made his point, sat back in his chair complacently enough, letting his eyes wander round the book-lined walls of the room. Presently his gaze became fixed on a particular point just behind the detective's left shoulder. He stared at it with peculiar intensity, his face alive with sudden interest; but when Rogers turned to look in the same direction he saw nothing but a crowded shelf of books, indistinguishable from any other in the room, save for the unimportant matter of their titles.

'Dr Bottwink!' said Rogers loudly.

The historian started guiltily.

'I beg your pardon,' he said. 'I was temporarily abstracted. You were saying?'

'Have you seen this before?'

From somewhere the detective had produced a small crumpled screw of tissue paper. Spreading it out carefully on his knee, he revealed a few white crystals within. Dr Bottwink adjusted his spectacles and examined it carefully.

'No,' he said deliberately, 'I have not. What is it?'

'That will be for the analyst to say – when I can get at an analyst.'

'Quite so. Meanwhile, I would suggest that it would be unwise to attempt any amateur test of its nature, certainly not by taste. May I ask where it was found?'

'Under the card table.'

'I see. That would, of course, be consistent with—'

'With what?'

'With somebody having emptied the contents of this paper into Mr Robert's glass while it stood on the table, whether that somebody was himself or another. If it was another, we were all so occupied by his antics at the window that it might easily have been done without it being noticed. On the other hand, if he did it himself – but bah! Sergeant, need we keep up this farce any longer?'

'What do you mean?'

'I mean that you do not believe, any more than I believe, that this unfortunate individual destroyed himself. Does a man, however drunken, declare in public that he is about to make an important announcement and then take poison before he can deliver it? It is absurd. You have not asked me a single question about the facts of last night, and that can only be because you have already ascertained them from the others who were present, and in so doing destroyed this ridiculous conspiracy between Sir Julius and the rest. You have merely been testing me to see if I was in the conspiracy or not. Is it not so?'

'I am not here to answer your questions, Dr Bottwink.'

'As you please. But one question I should like answered very much, because it puzzles me. Have you found out what was the announcement Mr Robert was about to make, and if so, what was it?'

'I am not going to tell you that either.'

'A pity. If I knew that, it would perhaps help me to help you, and, believe me, I should like to help you if I could. Well, Sergeant, is there any other question you wish to put to me?'

'Just two more questions, sir, and then I shall not need

to trouble you again – for the present. You told me when I first saw you just now that you have an appointment to see Lord Warbeck. What was the nature of that appointment?'

'That is easily answered. It was not an appointment exactly, but Briggs informed me at breakfast that it was his lordship's desire to meet all his guests in his room this morning to wish them the compliments of the season. Considering what we knew and he did not, it must have been a rather painful affair, but I had no wish to avoid my share in it.'

'In fact, you did not see Lord Warbeck this morning?'

'No, of course not.'

'Neither before breakfast nor since?'

'But no! Even such an alien as myself, Sergeant, would know sufficient to be aware of the impropriety of greeting an English gentleman before breakfast. And after, I can assure you that I went straight to the muniment room and remained there until you came. But why do you ask?'

'Somebody,' said Rogers gravely, 'somebody visited his lordship in his room between the time that Briggs brought him his tray and the time that he went to clear it away again.'

Dr Bottwink said nothing. His eyebrows were two half-circles of interrogation, his mouth a little round O of surprise.

'Somebody,' the detective went on, 'had broken to him the news of his son's death. When Briggs went in to him the second time, he found him in a state of complete collapse.'

'And so he is dead, the poor fellow?'

'No. He is still alive, but no more than just alive. I can't tell whether he will be living by the time we can get a doctor to see him, or whether a doctor can do anything for him when he does come, but I should doubt it.'

'So!' said Dr Bottwink softly, half to himself. 'It is as one might expect. Yes, I find that very logical. And your second question, Sergeant?' he went on aloud.

'Just this. What were you looking at just now that interested you so much in this room?'

'I am glad you asked me that. I said that I wished to help you, did I not? Well, I was looking at a book that put me in mind of something not without significance, perhaps. I am looking at it now.'

He rose from his chair and walked across the room to a bookcase in the corner.

'This book,' he said, laying one finger on a small volume bound in green. 'The life of William Pitt, by Lord Rosebery. A slight work, but by no means a superficial one. It treats of the younger Pitt, you understand, the second son of the Great Commoner. You should read it, Sergeant.'

'Thank you, sir,' said Rogers dryly, 'but at the moment I am concerned with the death of Robert Warbeck and not with the life of William Pitt.'

'It is a little out of my strict period,' Dr Bottwink went on, unheeding, 'and so I am not ashamed to say that I cannot give you the precise date, but I think it was 1788 or 1789. I know that you will find it in Rosebery, at all events. It is not anything that happened in that year that is important, you must understand, but something that did not happen. And that was very important indeed. Like Sherlock Holmes's dog in the night. You are not interested, Sergeant Rogers? The absent-minded professor is simply behaving in character, you think? I am sorry for it. At least I have done my little best to help. Have I your leave to go?'

XII

The Bedroom and the Library

Absolute stillness surrounded the rambling old house. Not a breath of wind rose to stir the dense fog which had settled over the snowbound countryside. Not a sound penetrated through the freezing air. Peering from the high window of Lord Warbeck's bedroom, Camilla Prendergast looked out into a world in which life itself seemed at a standstill – a world featureless, colourless and, to all appearance, boundless. It was difficult to believe that beyond that blank expanse the business of living still went on; that in crowded sea-lanes about the coast, ships crept cautiously through the murk, or swung at anchor, calling dismally to one another with their raucous sirens; that all over England, defying frost and snow, men and women were gathered together to keep Christmas in a spirit of love and happiness. Still harder was it to realise that this utter isolation was only momentary, the transient creation of a freak of Nature, and that within a matter of days, perhaps of hours only, it must vanish and leave Warbeck Hall and all that had happened there a focus of the busy, inquisitive attention of the outer world.

She shivered, and, turning on the window-seat where she sat, looked across the room. Here, save for the ticking of the clock upon the mantelpiece, it was as quiet and still as it was outside. Lord Warbeck lay upon his bed, his face hardly less white than the pillow, his shallow breathing barely stirring the coverlet. He had lain so all the morning, beyond speech or understanding, in his own isolation, within the larger isolation of his surroundings. When Briggs had reported the condition in which he had found him, Camilla had consented to sit with him, much as one might agree to watch by the dead, for there was nothing that she or anyone of those in the house could do to aid him.

She rose, went over to the bed, and bent over the still figure. It seemed to her that the face was, if anything, a shade paler, the respiration still fainter, but it was hard to detect degrees in vestiges of life so small. It was enough that he still lived. She stood looking intently at the thin, worn features for a time and then turned away. As she did so, the door behind her opened quietly and Briggs came into the room.

'How is his lordship?' he asked.

'There doesn't seem to be any change in him,' she replied. 'Briggs, how long will this go on, do you think?'

'I am sure I couldn't say, my lady,' said the butler, in the smooth monotone that he would have employed to answer any question about his household duties. 'I came to say,' he went on, without change of expression, 'that I shall be serving luncheon in a quarter of an hour.'

'I shan't want any lunch.'

'If I may say so, my lady, we ought all to keep our strength up. I think that you should eat something.'

'Then can't you send me up something here, Briggs? I can't leave his lordship in this state.'

'With respect, my lady, you ought to think of yourself.

It's not possible for you to stay cooped up here the whole day. Besides, there's no question of leaving his lordship alone. I have arranged for another person to sit with him.'

The strain of solitude had made Camilla sensitive to shades of expression which would otherwise have passed her by, and she caught him up quickly.

'Another person?' she repeated. 'Who do you mean? One of the servants?'

'Not a servant exactly, my lady. My daughter is here, and she is prepared to relieve your ladyship for the time being.'

'Your daughter? How odd, Briggs, I had quite forgotten that you had any family! Where is she?'

'In the corridor outside, my lady. She is quite dependable, I can assure you.'

For the first time Camilla's lips curved in a faint smile.

'She would hardly be your daughter if she wasn't,' she said. 'I'd like to see her.'

Briggs went to the door and reappeared immediately.

'My daughter Susan, my lady,' he said.

'How do you do?' said Lady Camilla, in the slightly exaggerated tone of politeness that well-bred women employ towards their social inferiors.

'How do you do?' said Susan. There was an undertone of defiance in her voice, and Briggs clicked his tongue in disapproval as he noted that no 'my lady' followed the form of words.

Without knowing why, Camilla felt suddenly that she was in the presence of an antagonist. This was very far from being the 'dependable' girl she had expected. Instead, here was a woman in whose bearing she detected some pent-up emotion that seemed in an odd way directed against herself. She had intended to do no more than greet the new-comer and pass on, but now she felt impelled to stop and discover what lay behind that strange expression, which seemed at once provocative and afraid. It was a strange little scene. Over and above any considerations of good manners, the convention of the sickroom was strong upon all three of them, and everything that was said was in a subdued tone, out of deference to the unseeing, unhearing patient on the bed.

'We haven't met before, have we?' Camilla said.

'No, we haven't.'

'You don't live here, do you?'

'No. I only came down a day or two ago.'

'I see. You've kept her very quiet, Briggs.'

'Dad didn't want anyone to know I was here.'

Briggs began to say something, but Susan forestalled him.

'People will have to know sooner or later, Dad. Why not now?'

Camilla looked from one to the other in bewilderment.

'I don't understand what all this is about,' she murmured. 'What is there to know?'

'Please pay no attention to her, my lady,' Briggs interposed, obviously distressed. 'I shouldn't have allowed her to come here if I'd thought— Susan, you had no call to speak to her ladyship in such a way.'

'I've a right to speak as I like. What's more, I've a right to be here,' Susan insisted. 'Which is more than some can say.'

'Susan!' Briggs protested. 'You told me you wouldn't make any trouble while his lordship—'

'Don't interrupt her, Briggs,' said Camilla loftily. 'I want to get to the bottom of this. What is this right you speak of?'

Susan's hand was fumbling in the pocket of her handbag. It came out gripping a closely folded piece of paper.

'That's what I mean,' she said abruptly, and thrust it into Camilla's hand.

Camilla unfolded the paper slowly. Slowly she read it through. Then, equally deliberately, she refolded it and gave it back to Susan. Her expression did not change and her voice remained subdued to the pitch proper to a sickroom as she said, 'Thank you. It is a great pity nobody knew of this before. It might have made a lot of difference to a good many people.' Turning to Briggs, she went on, 'Your daughter is quite right. She is entitled to be here. I shall lunch downstairs.'

Susan opened her mouth to say something, but before she could speak Lady Camilla had walked from the room. Her head was held high, and her bearing would have defied anyone to guess the blow her pride had received at the sight of the certificate of marriage, dated a year earlier, between Robert Arthur Perkin Warbeck, bachelor, and Susan Annie Briggs, spinster.

Briggs looked after her in silence. When she had gone he rounded on Susan.

'If I'd thought you'd forget yourself like that, my girl, I'd never have let you come here,' he said reproachfully.

'Why shouldn't I say what I like to her?' said his daughter, with an air of defiance that did not escape being at the same time defensive. 'I am as good as she is, aren't I?'

'No, my girl,' Briggs replied solemnly. 'Not if you was

to marry the highest in the land, you wouldn't be her equal, and it's no good your pretending otherwise.'

'We're not living in the Middle Ages now, Dad. Just because she's a lady born—'

'Just because she's a lady born,' repeated Briggs firmly, holding fast to his antiquated creed. 'You couldn't have walked out of a room like that – not if you tried for a thousand years. She's your superior, Susan – whatever she may have done.'

'Well, she—' Susan began hotly. Then she checked herself as she realised the significance of her father's words. 'What do you mean by that?' she said in a shocked whisper. 'Dad, you're not telling me that it was *she* that put that stuff in Robert's drink?'

'I'm not telling you anything – if only because I haven't anything to tell. I told Mr Rogers that it was suicide, though whether he believed me or not is more than I can say. Leave these things to those that they concern, I say. It can't alter your position now how it happened.' He looked at his watch. 'I've got to go now,' he said. 'There'll be a tray coming up to you directly. You've nothing to do but sit here quiet and let me know if his lordship – if anything happens. Haven't you brought any sewing or anything to keep you occupied?'

'I'll be all right,' said Susan, producing a manicure set from her bag. 'I shall do my nails. Funny thing, isn't it?' she added, as she settled down in an armchair. 'All this time, I've been wanting to get at his lordship, and now here I am at last, sitting in his room, when it's all over bar the shouting. Poor old man! He was nice, wasn't he?'

'Nice wasn't the word for him, my girl.'

'I expect he'd have been decent to me, if Robert had done the proper thing. It seems a shame I can't tell him. It's a rum set-up, isn't it? You trying to spare him and then his never knowing the one thing that might have cheered him up. Are you going to tell Sir Julius, Dad?' she added.

Briggs shook his head.

'He may call himself a socialist, but I bet it'll be a shock for him all the same,' Susan remarked. The idea seemed almost to put her in good humour, and she began operations on her finger-nails placidly enough as her father withdrew.

Sir Julius meanwhile was in the library. He entered it soon after Dr Bottwink had left it – so soon, indeed, that he might almost have been waiting outside the door for that very opportunity. He found Sergeant Rogers leaning back in an armchair smoking one of his homemade cigarettes, staring meditatively at the classic busts that surmounted the bookcases. Automatically, Rogers rose to his feet as the Chancellor of the Exchequer came in.

'Ah, Rogers,' said Sir Julius. 'Have you any news for me?'

'No, Sir Julius. I have tried the telephone again this morning, but it is still dead. We shall hear the weather report on the wireless at five minutes to one, and then we shall perhaps know how long these conditions are to last. They can't go on much longer, I should imagine.'

'I must get into touch with the Prime Minister at Chequers at the earliest possible moment. That is essential. I'm in a most difficult predicament, Rogers – most difficult.'

'Quite, sir.' Rogers displayed a notable lack of interest.

'Lady Camilla tells me that my cousin is in a very bad way.'

'Yes, sir. It would be interesting to know who it was who gave him the news that caused his collapse.'

'One of those damn fool servants, I suppose. They have no tact. If I had been left to break it to him, it might have been different. It is a terrible affair – terrible.'

'Quite, sir.'

'You wouldn't understand, Rogers, but I am very deeply concerned about Lord Warbeck's condition.'

'It is only natural that you should be, sir,' said the detective dryly. 'But you must remember that my concern at the moment is with Mr Robert Warbeck's death.'

Sir Julius's eyebrows shot up in surprise. 'But I thought that was settled,' he said. 'He killed himself. I explained it all to you this morning.'

'Yes, sir, you did. So did Mrs Carstairs and Briggs.'

'Well, there you are.'

'Unfortunately, Sir Julius, I have reason not to be satisfied with that explanation.'

'Not satisfied! When I told you what I had seen with my own eyes!'

'No, sir.'

'I know what it is, Rogers. You've been listening to that damned fellow Bottwink.'

'Sir Julius,' said Rogers seriously. 'You must remember, please, that I am now, at your own request, the detective officer investigating this case. I do not owe you any further duty than I do to any other witness in the matter. It is no part of my business to tell you where or from whom I have acquired my information. On the other hand, it is incumbent on you, just as much as on anyone else, to assist me by telling me the truth. And in order to help you to tell me the truth, I don't mind telling you this much: I have received three accounts of the circumstances in which Mr Warbeck is said to have committed suicide. They don't agree among themselves and they don't agree with my own observations on the spot. I do not believe any one of them. Now, sir, suppose we start again from the beginning and see if we can't get at the truth?'

Sir Julius had gone very red. He cleared his throat noisily, swallowed twice and then said:

'Very well, then. I did not see Robert put anything in his glass last night. That was a – an inexactitude. But apart from that, I have given you a full and accurate account of everything that occurred, so far as my observation went. I have nothing else to tell you.'

'Nothing, Sir Julius?'

'Absolutely nothing.'

The detective walked the length of the room and back again without speaking. Then he turned to Sir Julius and said, 'I was hoping, sir, that you would tell me something about your movements before dinner. You were in the neighbourhood of the pantry at one time, were you not?'

'I may have been.'

'Did you go into the pantry, by any chance?'

'I really can't recollect. I dare say I just looked in.'

'Was anybody else there when you just looked in?'

'I don't think there was.'

'Why should you, Sir Julius, be interesting yourself in the servants' quarters of the house?'

'I am very fond of this old place. It is a long time since

I have been here, and I took the opportunity to revive old memories.'

'Just as Mrs Carstairs did, apparently.'

'I know nothing at all about what Mrs Carstairs did. After all, I have an interest in the place. This is the home of my family, and I suppose I have a right to go where I like in it.'

'Your family – exactly, Sir Julius. And on Mr Robert Warbeck's death you stand next in succession to the peerage. Has that occurred to you?'

'Of course it's occurred to me,' retorted Sir Julius angrily. 'Who do you suppose wants to be a peer nowadays?'

'Did you know that Briggs kept cyanide of potassium in the pantry?'

'Certainly not. I shouldn't know the stuff if I saw it.'

'I see. Thank you, Sir Julius.'

Sir Julius did not take the opportunity to go. Instead he remained, shifting irresolutely from one foot to another, until he finally made up his mind to speak again.

'You mentioned Mrs Carstairs just now,' he said. 'Do I understand that she was also in the pantry yesterday evening?'

'It would seem so.'

'But that is absurd – that she should have had anything to do with poisoning Robert, I mean. I have known her for years – a most trusted and valued member of the Party. And she has no peerage to succeed to that I know of,' he added with a self-conscious little laugh. 'Why, I'd as soon think of suspecting Lady Camilla!'

He looked anxiously at the sergeant's face for a hint of

some reaction to his words, but there was absolutely no response from those stolid features.

'You can see how ridiculous the whole thing is,' he went on. 'It is perfectly plain to my mind that this was a case of suicide, even if it did not occur in exactly the way I – I fancied it did. It is so easy to be confused over details. If it was not, that only leaves Briggs – which is preposterous – and— Good heavens! Why did I not think of it before? Of course, Bottwink! Isn't the fellow a communist?'

'He does not admit to being one, Sir Julius.'

'Of course he doesn't. Fellows of that sort never do. But I remember the name now – he was involved in some sort of trouble in Austria before the war. It explains everything!'

'You mean that Mr Warbeck was killed because of his connection with the League of Liberty and Justice?'

'No, no!' protested Julius with rising excitement. 'The trouble with you policemen is that you don't understand anything about politics. Nobody in his senses cares anything about these absurd neo-Fascist societies. They're mere play-acting by half-witted children. No! Who are the real enemies of communism today? Why, we are – the democratic socialists of Western Europe! I was the person aimed at all the time! And the only thing that saved me was that in the confusion of the moment he put the poison into the wrong glass!'

'It is a theory certainly, Sir Julius,' said Rogers stolidly.

'And now that his attempt has failed he is trying to sow suspicion so as to discredit me – and through me, the cause of freedom throughout the world! I ask you, imagine the effect on Western Union if *I* were to be suspected of murder!'

To judge from his face at that moment, Rogers was incapable of imagination of any sort. All that he said was, 'I am bound to say, Sir Julius, that from what I have seen of Dr Bottwink, he seems to be more interested in eighteenth-century politics than modern ones.'

'Eighteenth-century fiddlesticks! I tell you, the man's a menace!'

'At all events,' said Rogers, 'I take it that you have now definitely abandoned your suggestion that this is a case of suicide?'

'Well – I – that is to say – I—' Julius stammered. 'Excuse me, but I think that is the gong for lunch!' And he bustled out of the room.

Left to himself, Rogers stood for a moment by the fireplace in meditation. Then he walked twice up and down the room, humming tonelessly under his breath. Finally, with a smile at his own weakness, he went to a bookcase and extracted a small green volume. He flicked rapidly through the pages, shrugged his shoulders and replaced it on the shelf.

XIII

A New Lord Warbeck

It was a gloomy little party that reassembled for lunch. Sir Julius took his place at the head of the table, with a malevolent look at Dr Bottwink, who sat on his right. Dr Bottwink, for his part, appeared quite at ease, but bore an abstracted look, as if his mind was still absorbed in the political issues of the eighteenth century. Mrs Carstairs, opposite, was nervous and fidgety. The place next to her was empty.

The meal began in silence, but it was not in Mrs Carstairs to keep quiet for long. Inevitably, she began to talk about the weather.

'How long will this go on, do you suppose?' she said. 'One feels so utterly *helpless,* being isolated in this way.'

Sir Julius, to whom, if anybody, the rather fatuous question was addressed, merely shook his head gloomily. Dr Bottwink, who was internally debating whether Wilkes really meant what he said in 1768, did not even hear it. In despair, Mrs Carstairs turned to Briggs.

'What do *you* think about it, Briggs?'

'I'm sure I couldn't say, madam.'

'But can't somebody do something about it? It seems so hopeless, just sitting here waiting for something to happen. Couldn't we organise a party to – to *do* something?'

'The farm-workers are trying to get through to the village, madam. They have made some little progress down the lane, I am informed, but the snow is becoming soft and they are having great difficulty.'

'Soft, did you say?'

'Yes, madam. There is apparently some prospect of a thaw.'

'Thank Heaven for that!'

'Quite, madam. Widespread floods are now anticipated by the wireless.'

Dr Bottwink had settled the problem of John Wilkes to his satisfaction in time to hear the last remark. Whether the look of pain with which he greeted it was inspired by a horror of floods or by disapproval of Briggs's choice of words remained his own secret.

'Thaw!' exclaimed Sir Julius. His eyes lighted up for an instant, but it was for an instant only. Then he relapsed into his former moroseness and resumed his meal in silence.

Lady Camilla came into the room at that moment, and Mrs Carstairs turned to her.

'Camilla, dear, do you hear that?' she exclaimed. 'It is going to thaw!'

'It was bound to sooner or later, I suppose.' Camilla took her seat at the table. Her face was composed, but there was a tell-tale touch of redness in her eyes. 'I'm sorry I'm late for lunch,' she went on. 'I'm glad you didn't wait for me.'

'But of course, Camilla, we should not have started without you if we had known you were coming down, should we, Sir Julius? I thought you would still be in Lord Warbeck's room. You haven't left him alone, have you, Camilla? After all, one doesn't know what might happen. Perhaps I'd better – I don't really want any lunch—'

Mrs Carstairs was about to rise from the table, but Camilla forestalled her.

'It is quite all right, Mrs Carstairs,' she said. 'Naturally, I haven't left him alone. There is someone looking after him.'

'But who, dear? I don't want to say a word against any of the servants – Briggs will appreciate that – but in the circumstances don't you think that one of us—'

Briggs was handing a dish to Camilla at the moment. She looked up at him as he did so, and a quick glance passed between them.

'You needn't worry,' she said swiftly. 'Briggs has been good enough to arrange that his daughter should sit with him until I can get back.'

'Your daughter, Briggs! But I seem to remember her. She was a little red-haired girl in the days when I took the Sunday school in the village. Why didn't you tell me she was here?'

Briggs did not reply immediately and the flow of reminiscence went on.

'She went into service in London, I remember, just about the time I married. Susan Briggs! Such a bright little thing, she was, but rather a handful! What became of her, Briggs? What is she doing now?'

'But I've just told you, Mrs Carstairs,' Camilla put in, her voice nervous and high-pitched. 'She is with Lord Warbeck while I am having my lunch.'

'I didn't mean that, of course, dear. I was only asking—'

Briggs, who had retreated to the sideboard, said impassively, 'My daughter, madam, was married. She has recently been widowed.'

'Dear me, how sad!'

'Quite, madam. There are hot mince-pies and cold plum pudding. Which would you prefer?'

Nobody can sustain a one-sided conversation with a butler indefinitely, and Mrs Carstairs gave in. Before she had had time to eat more than half a mince-pie, however, the silence of the room was disturbed by a hurried knocking on the door. Briggs opened it and immediately went out, closing it carefully behind him. He was absent for a few moments and then returned. Going up to the head of the table, he said:

'Sir Julius, would you mind coming out for a few moments?'

Murmuring an apology, Julius in his turn hurried out, followed by the butler. Their departure was followed by an uneasy silence.

'What has happened, do you suppose?' said Mrs Carstairs at last.

'I suppose,' said Dr Bottwink, speaking for the first time, 'that there is now a new Lord Warbeck.'

Dr Bottwink was right. The first words spoken to Sir Julius by Briggs when he was outside the dining-room were, 'He's gone, sir.'

'Gone?'

'Yes, Sir Julius. Quite peaceful, my daughter says.' Unashamedly Briggs produced a handkerchief and mopped his eyes. 'You – you'll want to come upstairs and see him, sir?'

'Yes,' said Julius heavily. 'I suppose I should.'

The two men climbed the stairs in silence. Briggs opened the door of Lord Warbeck's room and stood on one side for Julius to enter, but Julius, with an unusual appreciation of the feelings of another, took him by the arm and they entered together. They stood side by side looking down on the still, impassive face. There was nothing to be said. Lord Warbeck was finally out of this world, and, if his expression was any guide to the emotions with which he had left it, he was not sorry to be so.

When, some minutes later, they left the room, it was to find Susan standing outside. Julius did not seem to notice her, but Briggs stopped him as he was about to walk past.

'This is my daughter, Sir Julius,' he said.

'Ah, yes,' said Julius kindly. 'You were with him when he died, were you not?'

'Yes.'

'Did he – was he in a condition to say anything at the end?'

'Yes,' said Susan. There was a trace of eagerness in her hard, flat voice. 'I was wanting to tell you. Just before he went off he seemed to come to, all of a sudden, just for a moment or two, sort of, and he said quite distinct, "Tell Julius I'm sorry." That was what he said. "Tell Julius I'm sorry." Then he gave a kind of shudder and it was all over with him.'

'Thank you,' said Julius. He turned to Briggs. 'That was very characteristic of my cousin,' he observed. 'He was a kind-hearted, considerate man to the last.'

'Of course I don't know what he meant exactly,' Susan went on. 'But—'

'No, no, my girl. Of course you wouldn't. But I understand, perfectly. I am very glad you gave me his message.'

He was about to move away when Susan spoke again.

'There was something else I had to tell you that's a lot more important,' she said.

Julius was tired and depressed, and Susan's familiar manner grated on his overwrought nerves.

'Whatever it is, I am sure it can wait for a little,' he said rather shortly. 'I have a great deal to think of at the moment, you must realise that. Briggs, will you—?'

'I think, sir,' said Briggs, 'that it would be as well if I were to explain matters. As my daughter here says, it is a matter of importance.'

'I'd rather explain it myself,' Susan put in. 'It's my business after all, and I shan't waste the time you would.' She turned to Julius. 'This is all it is: you came out of that door a minute ago thinking that now the old gentleman's dead you were Lord Warbeck. Well, you're not.'

Julius stared at her in complete bewilderment.

'Not Lord Warbeck?' he faltered. '*Not* Lord Warbeck?'

He turned to Briggs as though for assurance that he was not dreaming.

'What my daughter says is quite correct, Sir Julius,' Briggs assured him. 'Mr Robert was married to her, entirely without my knowledge or consent, I need not say, and—'

'And my baby boy is the rightful Lord Warbeck!' exclaimed Susan in the tones of the heroine of an old-fashioned melodrama.

'You – you have a boy – a son?' stammered Sir Julius. 'Robert's boy? Born in wedlock? Good Heavens! I never dreamed – I always thought – I—'

Quite without warning, he fainted.

*

137

When he came to, Sir Julius found himself looking up into the anxious face of Briggs, who was bending over him. Susan had disappeared.

'Are you all right, sir?' the butler asked.

'Yes, yes, I shall be all right in a minute. Help me up on to that chair, Briggs . . . That's better. Get me a glass of water . . . Thanks. Now tell me, what happened? Was I unconscious long?'

'Only for a moment or two, Sir Julius. I am afraid you fell somewhat heavily.'

Julius rubbed the back of his head reflectively.

'I certainly did,' he remarked.

'I am sorry, sir. I had no time to catch you. It was all so sudden. I fear that this has been rather a shock to you.'

'I have had a good many shocks in the last twenty-four hours.'

'I regret very much that my daughter should have acted so – so crudely, Sir Julius.'

To Briggs's astonishment, Julius began to laugh. Having once begun, he seemed unable to stop. His hand, which still held the glass of water, shook so much that the water spilled over on to the floor.

'Take the glass, Briggs, for God's sake!' he spluttered.

'Yes, Sir Julius, of course,' said the butler, by now thoroughly alarmed. He rescued the glass and stood looking solicitously at him while the fit of unnatural mirth took its course. Presently it stopped as abruptly as it had begun.

'Don't blame your daughter, Briggs,' said Sir Julius, wiping his eyes. 'From her point of view, her attitude is perfectly natural.'

'Possibly, Sir Julius, but I deprecate it none the less.'

'This is all true, I take it? I haven't dreamt it? It still seems to me quite incredible.'

'I assure you that it is perfectly true, Sir Julius.'

'And how do you like being the grandfather of a peer of the realm, Briggs?'

'I regard it as a great misfortune, sir, to a man in my station.'

The reply seemed likely to set Julius off laughing again, but he checked himself.

'Did he – my cousin – know anything about it?' he asked.

'No, indeed, Sir Julius. It was scarcely a matter that I could discuss with him. I was, of course, relying on Mr Robert to put things right with his lordship.'

'A great mistake to rely on Robert for anything,' said Julius soberly. 'That child has a better man for his grandfather than his father would have ever been.' He rose heavily to his feet. 'I must go down to the others,' he went on. 'They will be wondering what has become of me.'

'You are sure you are yourself again now, Sir Julius?'

'Yes, I can manage all right. It was only a momentary faintness. Perhaps you had better give me your arm, though. And I'd just as soon you didn't mention anything about this to anyone.'

'I was about to ask you the very same thing, Sir Julius.'

'For a man in my position,' Julius went on, as they walked down the stairs together, 'it is just as well for there to be no gossip about questions of health and so forth. It puts ideas into people's heads. I am a perfectly fit and strong man, normally. It is most unlike me to be overcome in this way – quite unprecedented, I may say. But if irresponsible suggestions were made that I was failing, it might do great harm. You follow me?'

'Quite, Sir Julius. It would never occur to me to speak about it to anyone. But that was not what I had in mind, exactly.'

'Eh?'

'I was going to ask you, sir, to be good enough not to say anything for the time being about – about my grandson, sir.'

Julius stopped short and looked at him in astonishment.

'But why on earth not, man?' he demanded.

'Well, sir, I feel myself in a somewhat embarrassing position, if I may put it that way.'

'If it comes to that, you're not the only one. You can't seriously hope to hush a thing like this up, you know.'

'Of course not, Sir Julius, I fully realise that. It is only that I would be happier if it were not generally known until the house-party had dispersed. I should not like to appear before Mrs Carstairs and Lady Camilla as a member of the family, if you follow me, sir. It would hardly be proper. Lady Camilla is already aware of Mr Robert's misalliance, unfortunately, and it was very upsetting for us both. If you could see your way to say nothing further on the subject, sir, I should be very much obliged.'

Julius hesitated some time before he replied. When he did speak something of the geniality in his manner had disappeared.

'Is that your only reason for not wanting to reveal this very important fact?' he said.

'Sir?'

'Has it not occurred to you that Sergeant Rogers might also be interested in it?'

'I don't see that it concerns Sergeant Rogers in any way, sir.'

'Don't you, Briggs? Just think. Just before he died Mr Warbeck was on the point of making what he called an important announcement. Sergeant Rogers asked me if I knew what it was about. Did he not put the same question to you?'

'Yes, Sir Julius, I must admit that he did.'

'It is pretty obvious to me now what that announcement was to have been. You didn't tell him, did you, Briggs?'

'In the circumstances, Sir Julius, I did not consider it necessary.'

'Or was it because you had something to conceal?'

'Really, sir, I'm sure I don't know what to say when you make a suggestion like that. It's – it's really not what I would expect, coming from a gentleman like yourself.'

'Let's forget the gentleman business for a moment. Rogers has already been good enough to hint that I may have had a motive for murdering Mr Warbeck. I don't see why you should put yourself in any better position than I am in. This is a case of each man for himself, Briggs, and if you don't make a clean breast of it to the police I shall have to give them the information in my own interests.'

Briggs gulped nervously, and then said, 'Very good, Sir Julius, I shall see the sergeant straight away. I should point out, however—'

'Yes?'

'Well, sir, I understood that we had agreed that Mr Robert committed suicide.'

'I think that you can forget that, Briggs. I am fairly sure you will find that Sergeant Rogers has.'

'Very good, sir. And so far as the ladies are concerned—?'

'You may rely on me, Briggs. I regard that as your own affair.'

Lunch had been finished some time when Julius finally re-entered the dining-room, but the party had not dispersed. He found them grouped together by the fireplace, a dejected, ill-assorted trio, bound together by a common anxiety. They turned towards him as he came in.

'Yes,' said Julius, answering the mute enquiry in their eyes. 'My poor cousin has passed away. His end was very peaceful.'

Nobody said anything for a moment. Mrs Carstairs drew a sharp breath that sounded almost like a hiss in the silence. Dr Bottwink, his hands thrust deep into his pockets, shook his head slowly from side to side. Then Camilla began to speak in a harsh, unnatural voice.

'That makes two of them,' she said. 'Robert locked away in the drawing-room and Uncle Tom in his bed upstairs. Just the four of us left! Four of us, shut in by this infernal fog and snow. Who'll be the next to go, do you suppose?'

'Camilla, dear,' exclaimed Mrs Carstairs. 'You mustn't talk like that! You're distraught! Of course we're all very sad about poor Lord Warbeck, but—'

'I want to get away from here,' went on Camilla, unheeding. 'I want to get away before it is too late. There is a curse on this house. It smells of death. We're not safe here – not one of us. Can't you feel that, any of you? Don't you understand that the longer we stay here—'

'As to staying here, my lady,' said Dr Bottwink in deliberately flat tones, 'it is unfortunately the case that we have no option in the matter until—'

He was interrupted by what sounded like a violent rapping on the window-pane. All turned at the sound, but it was Mrs Carstairs who first appreciated its significance.

'It's all right!' she cried in a voice that was suddenly gay and confident. 'Don't you see, Camilla? The fog is lifting and it has started to rain!'

XIV

Effects of a Thaw

'You ought to have told me about this in the first place,' said Rogers severely.

'Yes, Mr Rogers,' said Briggs in a humble tone, 'I quite see that now. But I'd got so into the habit of keeping quiet about it that it had become almost second nature with me, so to speak. You see, I looked on it as a matter between myself and Mr Robert.'

'Exactly. You thought that it was his duty to tell his father and to acknowledge your daughter as his wife?'

'Just so, Mr Rogers.'

'And you had been threatening him with the consequences if he didn't do so?'

'I don't like to use the word threaten, Mr Rogers. There were some hard words between us, that I will admit. But if it comes to threats, what could I do? If the worst came to the worst, I could tell his lordship, but in his state of health I wasn't going to be the one to give him a shock that might have killed him.'

'You were very fond of Lord Warbeck, weren't you?'

The butler nodded silently.

'And not particularly fond of his son?'

'He did not act like a gentleman, Mr Rogers, and that's a fact.'

'May it be that you preferred killing the son to shocking

your master?'

'And look what the shock of Mr Robert's death did to him, God rest him!' exclaimed Briggs.

The detective made no comment. He walked over to the window and stared out. Rain was lashing the panes, and even as he watched a great slab of snow slid from the roof and fell with a thud to the ground.

'You will have an opportunity of making your explanation to the Markshire police before very long,' he said. 'All right, Briggs, you can sign your statement and go. I suppose I had better take a statement from your daughter too, so as to have a complete file before I hand over.' He looked utterly weary and depressed.

'Very good, Mr Rogers, I will send Mrs Warbeck to you now.'

'Who? Of course, yes, I was forgetting. Tell me something before you go. If this rain stops soon, how soon do you reckon anybody will be able to get through?'

'It all depends on the Didder, Mr Rogers.'

'The what?'

'The Didder – the stream you have to cross to get to the village. Last time we had snow like this – that was in the old lord's time – we were cut off by floods for three days when the thaw came. But nowadays, what with Conservancy Boards and drainage schemes and things, the river runs away much quicker than it used to. In fact, his lordship always complains – did complain, I should say – that they've ruined the fishing between them. I'm hopeful, myself, that we shall be in touch with the outside world by tomorrow.'

'Tomorrow!' the sergeant echoed. He turned again to the

window, so that Briggs could not see the expression on his face. But his back betrayed him. The stalwart figure was sagging perceptibly and the broad shoulders had lost their square, confident outline. The silhouette against the light was that of a defeated, dispirited man, looking forward to tomorrow, when he must hand over to his professional rivals a case in which he had had to admit failure.

So far as the rest of the inhabitants of Warbeck Hall were concerned, the coming of the rain brought nothing but a blessed sense of relief. They stood together at the dining-room window, watching the white world outside transform itself before their eyes. The smooth coverlet that had masked lawns and flower-beds was already pitted by little dark holes. Vague hummocks of snow revealed themselves as rose-bushes. Wherever there was a depression in the ground, a dark, shallow pool began to form, widening and deepening as they looked. The air was filled with the heavy plash of water falling in cascades from the gutters of the roof.

'The pipes are still choked with snow,' remarked Julius. 'The attics will be all flooded at this rate.' But he made no move.

'I trust that the muniment room is watertight,' said Dr Bottwink. 'It would be a major disaster to scholarship if anything were to happen to the manuscripts there.' But even this thought could not tear him from the window.

'Isn't it a wonderful sight?' Mrs Carstairs breathed. 'It seems wrong to say so after all that has happened, but I feel almost happy at this moment.'

'Paradoxically enough,' said Dr Bottwink, 'now that the

whole visible world seems to be dissolving in water, I feel very much as the passengers on the Ark must have felt when the flood began to abate.' He sighed and added, 'It is unfortunate that we shall not, like them, emerge into a world in which all other life is extinct, but instead into one very thickly peopled with highly inquisitive individuals, who will put to us a great number of questions to which at the moment we have no answers.'

Nothing, Julius's expression said, could have been in worse taste than this observation. Its depressing realism certainly had the effect of stifling further conversation. For some time, however, they continued to stand looking out at the fascinating spectacle as the snow crumbled like a sand-castle before an advancing tide. Then Camilla uttered a huge yawn.

'God! I'm tired,' she said. 'I'm going up to my room to lie down. I think I could sleep now.'

Not long after she had gone the three watchers who were left became aware that the light in the sky was growing stronger. The clouds were thinning, the rain diminished to a mere drizzle, and there was a glimpse of a pale, dispirited sun.

'I'm going out,' Julius suddenly announced.

'Out!' exclaimed Mrs Carstairs. 'But, Sir Julius, that's impossible!'

'Nonsense! One can't stay shut up in here for ever. I want a breath of fresh air.'

'You will be up to your knees in water before you have gone a yard,' Mrs Carstairs objected.

'I shall borrow a pair of waders. Briggs will know where to find them. I shall stick to the drive, of course. If I can, I shall make my way towards the village. I may even be able to get across the bridge, and if so, I can send for help. It's worth trying anyway. At the worst, I shall have had some exercise.'

'You will be careful, won't you?' said Mrs Carstairs anxiously. 'After all that has happened, we can't face any more—' Her voice trembled. '– any more disasters. And your life is very precious to the country.'

'I can take care of myself,' said Julius in a confident tone. 'Ah, Briggs, there you are!'

'Yes, Sir Julius, I had come to clear away luncheon. I am afraid it has been much delayed, but—'

'Never mind it now. I'm going out, and I want you to find me his lordship's waders. The thigh-length pair will do . . .'

The two men left the room together.

'The new Lord Warbeck seems to be very cheerful and energetic all at once,' said Dr Bottwink, when he had gone. 'It's the reaction, no doubt. By the way, madame, I observed that you continued to address him as Sir Julius. Is that correct?'

'Quite correct – until the funeral.'

'I am obliged. There are *nuances* in these matters which are not easy for a foreigner to understand.'

'I think it is a great pity that you foreigners concern yourselves so much with what is out of date in this country,' said Mrs Carstairs severely. 'As I think I have pointed out to you before, we are living in an advanced, democratic state, far more advanced in all the things that matter than any of your so-called people's democracies. Such things as titles and peerages are interesting relics of the past, no

148

more, and you would be far better occupied in studying our unrivalled system of social welfare, for example, than in brooding over trifles like the proper way to address a fellow citizen.'

'I stand corrected,' said Dr Bottwink humbly. 'I am, of course, aware that England has progressed in many ways towards egalitarianism. It is interesting, and perhaps at this moment pertinent, to observe that you have just the other day abolished the privilege of peers to be tried for murder by a different process of law to that employed for us humbler folk. None the less, to an outsider like myself, it would appear that in some respects you are still under the power of the dead hand of the past. I encountered a most interesting example of this only this morning. Perhaps you would like to hear it.'

Dr Bottwink suddenly realised that he was talking to an empty room. He sighed and turned away. In a few moments he was once more climbing the steep ascent to the muniment room where the unchanging past awaited him with all its treasures.

Wearing an old fishing hat of his cousin's, a mackintosh several sizes too large for him and a pair of waders and stout brogues, Julius splashed his way down the drive. Mud-coloured slush alternated with patches of soft snow into which he sank over his knees. The land-drains were choked and the ditches had spilled over into large yellow pools wherever there was a depression. But towards the farm, in the direction which he was taking, the general trend of the land was downhill; so that he was in effect walking most of the way along the bed of a shallow, fast-flowing river, travelling downstream. From his right, where the ground rose steeply, the melting snow was discharging a series of rivulets which had already scored deep channels in the gravel surface of the drive. To his left the overspill of water was plunging down to turn the meadow below into a quagmire. The snow was disappearing with astonishing rapidity. Already, he could see, there were one or two bare patches on the hillside to the right. He was puzzled that they showed up brown and not green, until, at a nearer approach, they proved to be composed, not of bare earth, but of hordes of famished rabbits, which had gathered there to feed on the newly exposed grass.

It was not easy walking, hampered as he was in his heavy gear, but Julius made good progress until he came in sight of the farm on his left. He did not approach the house but held straight forward towards the village. A man came out into the farmyard and shouted something as he passed. Julius waved to him and pressed on unheeding. He was sweating hard with the unaccustomed exercise. His face was scarlet with exertion. If it was a breath of fresh air that he had come out to seek, he had already achieved his purpose; but he plunged steadily onward, as though his life depended on it.

Rounding the farmyard wall, he was confronted with a short slope beyond which, he knew, the way led downwards again to the river and the village beyond. He saw at once what the man at the farm had been trying to tell him. The wind of the last two days had piled the snow in a deep drift against the slope, and here, before the advent of the thaw, the farm-hands had endeavoured to cut their way through to the outer world. He found himself walking up a narrow passage between banks of snow, higher than himself. They were oozing moisture at their base, but still stood, solid and compressed, hardly as yet affected by the rise in the temperature. It was slippery underfoot, where the snow had been hardened to ice by the coming and going of the men working there. Soon he was at the end of the cleared passage and had reached the point where work had been abandoned. Here his troubles really began. He was confronted with a wall of snow – not so very high, after all, three or four feet at the most, but a wall of rotting snow, quite different from the man-made banks which he had just traversed, a wall up which it was impossible to climb, through which it was well-nigh impossible to pass.

The Chancellor of the Exchequer attacked the obstacle with astonishing determination. At his first step he sank in almost to the full extent of his waders, at the second one of his brogues was nearly sucked off his foot. But still he persisted. Flailing with his arms to keep his balance, dripping wet within and without, he plunged into the soft, sticky mass. It was like wading in glue. For some time it seemed impossible to make any progress. Then, as he floundered desperately forwards, he came upon a patch of hard snow, a foot or so beneath the surface, which could support his weight. From then on, matters became easier. After what seemed an eternity of effort, he reached the end of the drift, the familiar landmarks of the railings bordering the drive reappeared on either side and he staggered up the last few yards of the slope to stand panting and victorious on the crest.

Julius mopped his streaming face with a soaked pocket handkerchief. Spots were dancing before his eyes, and it was not until after some time that he was able to focus his sight on the prospect that now opened up before him. Straight ahead, less than half a mile away, lay Warbeck village. On a little hillock, surrounded by trees, he could see the Norman tower of the church from which had sounded the chimes of the night before. A glint of light from the westering sun picked out the golden weathercock so plainly in the rain-washed air that it looked as if he had but to stretch out his hand to touch it. But between him and the village lay a turbid sheet of water, its dark surface dotted with white, where lumps of snow had floated out from the banks and been carried away by the swollen stream. A double line of pollarded willows marked the course of the river, but for a good hundred yards on either side of them the flood waters extended in a muddy lake. Immediately in front of him, he could see the hump-backed bridge that carried the road to the village, its arch still clear of the water, but the last stretch of the drive, where it traversed the low-lying water-meadows, had disappeared beneath the flood.

Julius took stock of the position. He could gauge the depth of the water ahead accurately enough from the fences on either side. So far as he could tell, it was not more than a foot or two at the most. Obviously, this great accumulation of water had come from the head waters of the stream, where the thaw must have begun several hours earlier than lower down the valley. The afternoon's rain could hardly yet have begun to have its full effect on the river's level. The melting snow was still discharging itself into the valley by a thousand drains and ditches. That meant that the Didder was still rising. If he did not get across now, he might be delayed indefinitely. Taking a deep breath, he strode on down the hill, the water squelching in his waders with every step. It was as he had expected. Not until he was within a few yards of the bridge did the water reach to his knees. At the same time, the current proved a good deal stronger than he had bargained for. Débris had partially choked the arch of the bridge, and spilled much of the main force of the stream over the near bank. As he advanced, he found it progressively more and more difficult to keep a straight course. He had omitted to bring a stick with him and as he approached his objective he could feel the water tugging at his feet, seeking to pluck him from his foothold. But there was firm ground beneath him, he was well shod, and by leaning over in the upstream direction he was able to maintain his balance well enough.

Then, quite without warning, his left foot plunged into a deep hole. He felt a sudden shock of cold as water poured in over the top of the wader. It flashed through his mind that the foundations of the drive must have been undermined by the flood. With a convulsive effort he brought his right foot forward and found a solid footing well within his depth. Laboriously he dragged the submerged foot out of the hole and brought it up beside the other. More than ever now did he regret the absence of a wading-stick. It was impossible to guess at the nature of the bottom beneath the muddy stream. On the other hand, to go back was as dangerous as to advance. The bridge rose invitingly before him, only a few strides away. Very cautiously, moving now only a few inches at a time, he began to shuffle towards it.

He had not gone more than a yard or so when the gravel

surface on which he was standing slid bodily away beneath him into the void. Sir Julius fell flat on his back. His head remained above the surface, but the rest of his body was completely submerged. At the same moment his feet were plucked from the ground and floated to the surface, the imprisoned air in the waders making them the only buoyant part of his body. By no conceivable effort could he now regain his feet. With the roar of the angry waters in his ears, he watched helplessly while the two air balloons on his legs spun round in an eddy and then set off downstream, dragging behind them a heavy water-logged, slowly sinking bundle that – it came to him with a sudden shock of terror – was really Sir Julius Warbeck, MP, now within measurable distance of death.

He was aware of a sudden sharp pain beneath his right armpit. For a blurred second or two he wondered whether this was a sensation of drowning hitherto unrecorded, and then the pain resolved itself into a tug. He realised that he was no longer floating with the current, but moving rapidly across it. Twisting his head round, he discovered the means of propulsion in a stout stick, the curved handle of which was fixed firmly under his upper arm. The other end was in the hands of Detective-Sergeant Rogers, who, standing comfortably in the shallows, was engaged in hauling him to shore with considerably less apparent emotion than most people display at gaffing a salmon.

Drenched, miserable and speechless, the Chancellor of the Exchequer allowed himself to be helped to his feet. Still speechless, he was guided to dry land and stood shivering while Rogers dumbly removed his brogues and waders, and emptied them of water. The yet more horrible moment arrived when he had to put the noisome, clammy things on again. It was at this point that he found his tongue.

'Rogers,' said Sir Julius, hopping on one stockinged foot, 'I am very much obliged to you.'

'Not at all, sir,' said the sergeant imperturbably. 'After all, it's my job.' He supported Julius with a massive arm, and added, 'In fact, if I hadn't fallen down on my job pretty badly, you wouldn't have been here at all. Allow me, sir.' He bent down to fasten the strap of a brogue.

'Personally, I think you did a pretty good job getting me out of that,' remarked Julius to Rogers's bent back.

The sergeant raised a face red from stooping. 'My job, sir,' he said severely, 'is looking after you. That's what I'm here for. If I hadn't allowed myself to get carried away, so to speak, trying to do something that rightly belongs to the Markshire police, I should never have let you get into such a pickle. Now, sir, if you're ready, we'll be getting back as soon as we can. You'd better take my arm, and we'll move as fast as we can manage. The sooner you're out of those wet things the better.'

Arm in arm the soaked pair staggered off. Sergeant Rogers permitted himself only one further reference to the adventure on the way.

'I should appreciate it, sir,' he said, 'if you did not report this matter to Special Branch. I shouldn't like it to be thought that I was so lacking in my duty as to let you go out alone on a day like this.'

'I'll do whatever you please about that,' said Sir Julius. 'But dash it, I am not a babe in arms. I am entitled to go out for a walk by myself if I want to. If I had got drowned it would have been my own fault.'

'Your fault, sir, and my responsibility. You forget that. And suppose you had not been drowned? I'm not sure that that wouldn't have been worse from my point of view. Suppose you had turned up in Downing Street tomorrow without me? I should have had a lot of awkward explaining to do.'

'Very true,' said Julius humbly. 'I am sorry, Rogers; it was selfish of me.'

'Just as a matter of interest, Sir Julius, I suppose it was Downing Street you were making for?'

Cold and exhausted though he was, Julius smiled. 'Oh yes,' he assured his companion. 'It was Downing Street. I'm not a fugitive escaping from justice, Rogers.'

'Ah,' said the detective. It was impossible to tell from his tone whether he believed the assertion or not. 'It's only a matter of academic interest for me now, as you might say, but I thought it would be interesting to know.'

XV

Dr Bottwink in Error

It was nearly dark when the two men arrived back at
Warbeck Hall in a renewed downpour of rain. Anybody
who had been there to see them might well have been
excused for thinking that their figures were indeed those
of a recaptured prisoner and his keeper. Sir Julius could
hardly drag one foot after another and could scarcely have
completed the journey but for the support of Rogers, who
marched impassively by his side, holding his arm in a firm
grip, a look of sullen determination on his face. But hap-
pily there was no-one to see the Chancellor's disgrace and
they gained a side entrance unobserved.

Still in silence, the sergeant led his charge to the cloak-
room, where he stripped him of his mackintosh and waders.
Sir Julius made no protest. In any case his fingers were by
now too numb for him to have dealt with the sodden straps
and buckles for himself. This done, he allowed himself to be
taken upstairs to his room and undressed. Meekly he swallowed the hot brandy and water that Rogers conjured up
with astonishing speed; meekly he got into the hot bath
that Rogers prepared for him. He was by now in such a state
of subservience that he felt positively grateful that the man
at least abstained from accompanying him into the bath-
room and scrubbing him down.

On emerging from his bath, he found Rogers waiting

for him in his room, having in the interval found himself a change of clothes. The bath and the drink had worked wonders, and Sir Julius was by now sufficiently recovered from his own discomfort to reflect that he was not the only person to have had a wetting that afternoon.

'I hope you are none the worse, Rogers,' he said in an unwonted tone of consideration.

'Thank you, no sir,' said the detective shortly, as if a trifle annoyed that any human weakness should be attributed to him. 'And now I dare say you would like to go to bed.'

'No, no. I am perfectly all right again, thanks to your attention, Rogers. I am a little tired and shall retire early, perhaps. But at the moment I am more in need of food than rest.'

'Very good, sir. In that case, as soon as you are dressed we will go down to tea.'

The 'we' was not lost on Sir Julius. He understood perfectly all that it implied. From now on Sergeant Rogers was to be his constant companion. So long as he remained at Warbeck Hall he would never be out of range of that cold, disapproving eye. With a sigh, he resigned himself to the inevitable and made haste to dress himself.

'Well, Sir Julius,' said Mrs Carstairs, as he and his keeper entered the library, 'here you are. Did you get very wet?'

Sir Julius was astonished to find that tea was only just being brought in. The whole of his escapade, during which he had lived through enough sensations to last a lifetime, had occupied little more than an hour. It was a relief to find that his absence had not been long enough to occasion remark. There was Mrs Carstairs, preparing herself to preside over the teapot, just as Camilla had done – could it be only twenty-four hours ago? – and Dr Bottwink, placid and silent, both of them completely unaware that he had done anything more than take a stroll in the rain. At the same time he felt a little aggrieved that after such a fearful ordeal he should be taken for granted. One does not narrowly escape from drowning every day. But much though he loved to talk about himself and his doings, this was an occasion for restraint.

'I did. Very wet indeed,' he replied. 'So did Sergeant Rogers, who came with me part of the way. Which reminds me, you have no objection, I hope, to Rogers joining us at tea? He feels that in all the circumstances it would perhaps be advisable—'

'Of course, of course.' Mrs Carstairs appeared to be in high good humour. 'We shall be delighted to have his company, shall we not, Dr Bottwink? (I've got the name right now, you see!) Briggs, will you fetch another cup and saucer for Sergeant Rogers?'

'Very good, madam.'

Briggs's voice was completely devoid of expression. By no movement of limb or feature did he give the smallest indication that the order was anything but a perfectly normal one. A well-trained butler is schooled to repress his feelings on such occasions. None the less, by some occult means he contrived to convey to every person in the room that he was outraged by the proposal. How he did it, it was impossible to say. Such subtle means of a communication are the secrets of telepathists and well-trained butlers.

As though in deliberate defiance of the waves of

disapproval directed at her, Mrs Carstairs chose to improve on the occasion.

'I quite understand, Sir Julius,' she said confidentially, 'and, if I may say so, I entirely approve. After all, you are a particularly important person just now, are you not?'

For the second time in less than a minute Julius found himself under the cruel necessity of holding his peace about the subject which, of all subjects under the sun, he most liked to discuss. That he succeeded on this occasion was perhaps due to the presence of Briggs, perhaps simply to the fact that Mrs Carstairs did not give him the opportunity to say anything. For in the next breath she succeeded in giving additional offence to an already deeply wounded man.

'And bring a tray for Lady Camilla, Briggs,' she went on. 'I don't expect she will wish to come down. I'll take her up her tea before I have my own.'

Dr Bottwink, Julius and Rogers simultaneously offered to spare her the trouble by assuming the burden of Camilla's tray. Briggs emphatically but wordlessly declared that it was the butler's business and nobody else's to take meals up to guests at Warbeck Hall; but Mrs Carstairs disregarded them all. Keeping up a flow of inconsequential chatter, she dispensed tea to the men until a tray complete with a freshly made pot of tea was produced.

'You men must look after yourselves until I come back,' she said archly. 'But I shan't be more than a minute or two.'

Decidedly Mrs Carstairs was in good humour. She was humming a tune under her breath as she tripped – it was the only word for it – to the door which Briggs, exuding disapproval, held open for her. If there was one person in that unhappy household who had recovered hope and spirit since the onset of the thaw, it was certainly she.

The three men, left alone, resumed their seats in a room that had suddenly become blissfully silent. Julius found himself to be ravenously hungry. He devoured two buttered scones and half a plate of bread and butter, before going on to make deep inroads on the Christmas cake. It was perhaps fortunate that Dr Bottwink had a small appetite, for Rogers, too, proved to be a hearty eater.

The meal was accomplished with the minimum of words. Julius was too much engrossed in feeding to wish to speak, and neither of the other two was normally given to small talk. Only when the teapot was exhausted and cigarettes produced did anything that could be called conversation begin, and then it was little more than a few desultory remarks from Dr Bottwink about the weather, responded to by grunts from Julius and more civil monosyllabics from Rogers.

A little later, leaning back in an armchair, his weary legs extended towards the fire, Julius was feeling much as in younger days he used to feel after a long day in the saddle. (The fact that in his twenties he had been a regular rider to hounds was one of the most jealously guarded secrets in the higher circles of the Party.) He was going to be confoundedly stiff tomorrow. Why hadn't Rogers put mustard in that bath? He hadn't told him to do so, but the fellow should have thought of it for himself. No, that was hardly fair. After all, he was a policeman, not a valet. He had done pretty well as it was. The Chancellor dozed for a moment, then jerked himself awake. This wouldn't do! There was work to do, awaiting him in his room. He had better make a start on it now. But he remained glued to his seat, and his eyes began to close again. They opened once more as he heard Dr Bottwink's voice, coming apparently from an immense distance:

'Mrs Carstairs has been gone a long time.'

Julius looked round at the devastated tea table. 'We haven't left her much to eat,' he observed with a huge yawn. 'Briggs will have to get her some fresh tea when she does come.'

Rogers said nothing. To judge by appearances, he, too, was not more than half awake. Considering the hour at which he had gone to bed that morning, he was perhaps to be excused, but Dr Bottwink frowned at him contemptuously.

'I distinctly understood her to say that she would not be more than a minute or two,' he said. 'She has been gone now at least five-and-twenty minutes. Do you not find it strange?'

Sir Julius's eyes closed again. 'I certainly find it very peaceful,' he murmured.

Dr Bottwink shrugged his shoulders impatiently. He was about to make some rejoinder when the door opened. It was not Mrs Carstairs who entered, however, but only Briggs, who began to clear away the tea.

'Briggs,' said the historian, 'do you know where Mrs Carstairs is?'

'No, sir. She went up to Lady Camilla's room. Has she not come down?'

'She has not come down and she has not had any tea,' said Dr Bottwink in an anxious tone.

Briggs contemplated the table in silence for a moment.

'Perhaps I had better make her a fresh pot,' he suggested. 'And cut some more bread and butter.'

'I see. Like Sir Julius, you consider that everything is to be made right by a fresh pot of tea. Myself, I do not think so. Already some things have happened in this house that are not to be cured by pots of tea. Perhaps this is another. I do not know. I hope only that I may be wrong.'

'What exactly are you getting at, Dr Bottwink?' It was Rogers who spoke, and there was no doubt that Rogers was now wide awake.

'I do not know what I am getting at, as you put it. Perhaps it is simply that my nerves are getting at me. Merely, I ask myself – why should it take Mrs Carstairs nearly half an hour to give tea to the Lady Camilla? Or conversely, why should it take the Lady Camilla nearly half an hour to receive tea from Mrs Carstairs? It seems strange to me, and in a household like this everything that is strange is alarming.'

'You are easily alarmed, sir.'

'Very,' said Dr Bottwink simply. He fidgeted uneasily, balancing first on one leg, then on another, before turning to Briggs again.

'You are positive Mrs Carstairs went to Lady Camilla's room?' he said.

'She went in that direction, sir.'

'And since then nothing has been heard from her, or—' He paused, and went on emphatically, '– or of the Lady Camilla?'

'No, sir.'

'She went up to her room after lunch, did she not? She has not since rung her bell, or made her presence there known in any way?'

'Not to my knowledge, sir.'

'Then, Briggs, will you do me the favour of going to her ladyship's room? Knock on her door, enter if necessary – after all, you will require to take her tea away – and satisfy yourself that – that she is all right?'

Briggs, the tea tray in his hands, looked at him in astonishment.

'I will do so if you think it desirable, sir. It is not my place to enter a lady's bedroom, but—'

'At least knock on her door and get an answer if you can,' said Dr Bottwink urgently. 'Go, Briggs, I beg of you!'

'Very good, sir.'

With obvious reluctance, the butler went out, bearing the tray before him.

'And now,' said Julius, lifting himself ponderously from his chair, 'perhaps you will have the goodness to tell me what all this is about?'

Dr Bottwink, who had been pacing the room in an access of nerves, stopped abruptly in front of him and threw out his arms.

'Sir Julius,' he said, 'you have told me more than once, I think, that I do not comprehend English ways and customs. But you also pointed out to me that what has happened in this house has been quite un-English. Therefore I think I have as much right as anybody to say what I believe to be the position, and why I am, as the good Rogers here puts it, easily alarmed. The position, as I see it, is this: there is a killer abroad amongst us, who has already struck once – indeed, as I think, in effect twice. I have determined in my own mind who that killer is, and if the sergeant had been content to follow my advice I think

164

he would have reached the same conclusion. Now—'

He stopped abruptly as Briggs re-entered the room.

'Well?' he asked. 'You have been to Lady Camilla?'

'No, sir,' said the butler calmly. 'It did not prove necessary. There is no cause for alarm. Mrs Carstairs found that Lady Camilla was still asleep when she went up to her. She therefore decided to take the tray prepared for her ladyship to her own room and have her tea alone instead of returning here. That is all.'

'So much for that!' said Julius with a snort.

'Mrs Carstairs told you this?' asked Dr Bottwink swiftly.

'No, sir. My daughter happened to be on the landing when Mrs Carstairs came out of her ladyship's room and that was the information she conveyed to her. She added that Lady Camilla was not to be disturbed. Will you be requiring me further, sir?'

'So!' Dr Bottwink turned to Julius, his normally placid features working with excitement. 'Sir Julius, I intend to disturb Lady Camilla myself at once, and I only pray that I may find her still open to disturbance!'

He pushed past the astonished Briggs and dashed from the room.

'I think we had better go with him, sir,' murmured Rogers to Julius, and pressed after him. Julius followed, and with Briggs in the rear they all mounted the stairs.

They came up with Dr Bottwink outside Camilla's room. He was listening intently at the door. Evidently hearing nothing, he knocked loudly. There was no reply. He paused for a moment, then flung open the door and strode into the room, the others following nervously at his heels.

Lady Camilla was on her bed, the eiderdown drawn up to her shoulders. She lay on her side, her face turned away from the intruders. A look of intense anxiety was on Dr Bottwink's face as he approached. He leaned over, seized her shoulder and shook it.

And Camilla started violently, sat up in bed and stared at him, bewilderment merging into indignation as she slowly awoke.

'What the hell—?' said Lady Camilla, in a voice still heavy with sleep.

'I do not know what to say,' said Dr Bottwink. 'I have been very foolish. I am ashamed.'

'For the matter of that, you've succeeded in making us all look pretty stupid,' said Julius. 'Four of us, trampling into a girl's room like that, waking her up and frightening her out of her life—'

'Do not rub it in, Sir Julius. I repeat, I am ashamed. I apologise to you all.'

They were speaking on the landing, whither they had withdrawn after having somehow or another succeeded in beating a retreat from the bedroom.

'I shall go now to the muniment room,' said Dr Bottwink, 'and continue my work. I should never have left it. I am good for one thing only. It is a mistake to interfere in what is not one's business. This shall be a lesson to me.'

'Just a moment, sir.' It was Rogers who spoke. 'I think you are forgetting that the matter that was worrying you in the first place has still to be cleared up.'

'I do not understand.'

'I thought that you were concerned because Mrs

166

Carstairs left the library for a few minutes and did not come back.'

'Ah, that!' The historian shrugged his shoulders. 'It was only because she went to the Lady Camilla that I was worried. I was not afraid for the safety of Mrs Carstairs, no!'

'Well,' said the sergeant imperturbably, 'I don't see why you should be concerned for the safety of one person more than another's. My job is the safety of Sir Julius, and I am not now particularly interested in anybody else's. But since we are here, I think it would be as well to knock on Mrs Carstairs' door and make certain that she is all right too.'

'As you please, Sergeant. I repeat, it does not concern me. But this time I shall save myself embarrassment by remaining outside.'

Sergeant Rogers walked woodenly down the corridor to the door of Mrs Carstairs' room. As Dr Bottwink had done, he listened for any sounds within. Like Dr Bottwink, he knocked, but twice, and even more loudly. Then he flung open the door.

Mrs Carstairs was not in bed. She was sitting in a chair, staring straight at the door with wide-open eyes. She was quite dead.

XVI

A Pot of Tea

'But no!' said Dr Bottwink wearily. 'It is impossible! By all the rules of logic and reason, it is impossible!'

'But it has happened, Dr Bottwink,' said Rogers.

The four men were huddled about the library fire. Under the impact of disaster, precedence was forgotten, and Briggs, uninvited, had sat down with the rest. He was ashen pale and his hands were shaking uncontrollably. Of the others, Julius seemed stupefied, his eyes glazed, his movements slow and halting. Bottwink had collapsed like a balloon suddenly deflated. Even his round, full cheeks sagged, and there was a yellowish tinge to them that had not been there before. As to Rogers, his face bore no expression except an immense fatigue. He rolled a cigarette, his fingers going about their task automatically, but when it was completed he made no attempt to light it. Instead, he remained staring at the little paper cylinder in his hand, as though wondering how it got there.

'The thing is so absurd!' Dr Bottwink protested almost querulously. 'Mrs Carstairs, of all people!'

'I don't understand you,' said Julius heavily. 'If there is a maniac in this house going about murdering people, is there any reason why Mrs Carstairs should have been safer than anyone else?'

'If there is a maniac, then there is no reason for anything. That is logical. That I can comprehend. But I have seen no signs of mania here. On the contrary. I have assumed a murderer who is sane, and on that assumption there were just two people, two only, whose lives I was prepared to consider secure – Mrs Carstairs and yourself, Sir Julius. But now—' He shrugged his shoulders and was silent.

'May I ask, sir, why you should choose to bring my name into the matter, on any assumption?' said Julius. 'Are you implying—'

'This is getting us nowhere,' Rogers interposed. 'Let us stick to the facts. Mrs Carstairs has died, apparently in exactly the same way that Mr Robert Warbeck died – from cyanide poisoning.'

'There is no question that it was cyanide,' Dr Bottwink murmured.

'An analysis will have to be made in due course,' the detective went on, 'but all the evidence points to her having taken the poison in her tea. We know that there is a bottle of this poison somewhere in the house, but although I have searched her room thoroughly I have been unable to find it there. We can assume, therefore, that it was not self-administered. In that case, the poison was in the tea before Mrs Carstairs brought it into her room.'

Rogers paused and cleared his throat. As he went on in his flat, tired voice, Briggs began to tremble violently.

'We know something of the history of that tea,' he said. 'It was made, not for Mrs Carstairs, but for Lady Camilla Prendergast, and taken up to her room by the deceased. Apparently, it was only the chance that Lady Camilla was asleep that induced Mrs Carstairs to drink it herself, instead.'

'But why should she have done that?' Dr Bottwink broke in. 'Her own tea was waiting for her here. It seems to me most unnatural—'

'I am dealing simply with the facts,' said Rogers coldly. 'I have not yet seen Lady Camilla about this, but if she was in truth asleep when Mrs Carstairs came to her room, as she certainly was when we came to it, the facts seem to be pretty clear. From this it follows that if the tea was deliberately poisoned, it was intended to kill not Mrs Carstairs but Lady Camilla. Now the tea was freshly made in the kitchen—'

'I swear to God, sir, I never put anything in it!' cried Briggs.

'Made in the kitchen,' Rogers repeated inexorably. 'Brought in here by Briggs and handed to Mrs Carstairs. So far as we know, it never left her hands until she died. Briggs,' he turned abruptly to the white-faced butler, 'you made the tea, did you not?'

'Yes, Mr Rogers,' said Briggs in a voice hardly above a whisper. 'That is, I – yes, I made it.'

'Was anybody else with you at the time? The cook, where was she?'

'She and the rest of the staff were taking their tea in the housekeeper's room. I – I was quite alone.'

Rogers gave him a look of infinite weariness in which seemed to hide a touch of compassion.

'You had better tell the truth, you know,' he said. 'Who was with you in the kitchen?'

After a few seconds' silence that seemed to last a very long time, Briggs said in a strangled voice, 'My daughter was with me for part of the time.'

There was another silence, during which Rogers seemed to become aware once more of the cigarette in his hand. He smoothed out its crumpled exterior, put it in his mouth, lighted it and blew out a cloud of acrid smoke before asking, 'What part did she take in the tea-making?'

The men circled round the fire had to strain their ears to catch the reply. Briggs's head was sunk on his chest and his voice hardly rose above a whisper, as the words came tumbling helter-skelter from his pale lips.

'I was cutting the bread and butter at the kitchen table,' he said, 'when my daughter came into the room. The kettle was on the range behind me and just coming to the boil. She asked me who the tea was for and I told her. I'd warmed the pot and put the tea in it all ready, out of the same caddy you had yours in here from. Then the kettle boiled and she asked me should she fill the pot. To save myself trouble, I told her, yes. I didn't so much as look round. She filled the pot and put it on the tray beside me and went out. That's all, gentlemen.' He stopped abruptly and covered his face with his hands.

'But still I say it is impossible!' Dr Bottwink exclaimed.

'Thank you, sir,' Briggs murmured faintly. Then he rose stiffly to his feet.

'If you will excuse me,' he said, 'I will retire now. I have a good deal of work to do, and—'

'Just a moment, Briggs,' said Rogers. 'Before you go, there is another matter I want to ask you about. It was you who told us in the first place that Mrs Carstairs had taken the tea intended for Lady Camilla to her own room. You had that information from your daughter?'

'Yes, Mr Rogers. I reported it to you just as she told me.'

'Your daughter seems to have been very much concerned in this affair.'

'I – I can't believe that she had anything to do with it, Mr Rogers.'

'That is a matter she will have to explain to the proper authorities in due course. Where is she at this moment?'

'In her room, I believe. Do you wish to see her?'

The detective hesitated for a moment. 'Yes,' he said finally. 'Ask her to come down here at once. And you are to tell her nothing of what has occurred, do you understand?'

'Very good, Mr Rogers.'

After Briggs had gone Rogers turned to Julius.

'As I told you this afternoon, Sir Julius,' he said, 'my business here is to protect you. I do not regard myself any longer as in charge of this case. It cannot be long now before the local police arrive, and it will be their business to carry out the investigations. But I think it my duty as a police officer to give them as full a report of the facts as I can. That is the only reason why I propose to interview this young woman. I take it you have no objection?'

'Take your own course,' said Julius shortly.

'Would you mind very much,' put in Dr Bottwink, 'if I were to be present when you see this young person? It would interest me greatly.'

'Provided you do not try to take any part in the interview, sir, I can agree to that.'

'I am very much obliged. It puzzles me to think what interest the good Briggs's daughter should have to seek to poison Lady Camilla.'

'Motive enough,' grunted Julius. 'Two women and one

man.' He rose to his feet. 'I'm going up to my room,' he announced.

Rogers looked troubled.

'I am not sure, Sir Julius, that I ought to allow you—' he began.

'– to get out of your sight, you mean? I'll take care of myself. I'll lock my door behind me.' And before the sergeant could intervene he was gone.

'Two women and one man,' murmured Dr Bottwink, as the door closed behind him. 'That is a complication, certainly. I admit that I had not envisaged that. Do you agree with that theory, Sergeant Rogers?'

Rogers looked more exhausted than ever as he replied, 'I am not now concerned with theories, sir. My function is simply to assemble all the facts that come under my notice and hand them over to the proper quarter.'

'Ah, facts, yes! Perhaps that is the better course – if you can keep to it. Myself, I find it impossible to avoid ratiocination, and that is tiresome, particularly when it leads one to absurd conclusions. But speaking of facts, there was one small fact about Mrs Carstairs which you did not mention just now in your admirable *résumé* of the matter.'

'Yes?'

'I dare say it is quite without significance, but did you observe that her shoes were wet?'

'I did. There were traces on the carpet which indicated that she had been to the french window in her room and stepped out on to the balcony for a moment. There is a great deal of melting snow there still.'

'I am obliged. You have established the fact that

173

explains the condition, though not the reason that explains the fact. That you leave to others, as is proper. There is much to be said for the principle of the division of labour, is there not?'

The question did not seem to the sergeant to call for an answer, and nothing further was said between them until a few moments later Susan came into the room.

'You wanted to see me?' she said curtly.

'I did, yes. Won't you sit down, Mrs Warbeck?'

'*Lieber Gott!*' exclaimed Dr Bottwink.

'Dr Bottwink,' said Rogers severely, 'if you are going to remain here, you must not interrupt.'

'I apologise deeply, Sergeant. It will not occur again, I promise you.'

Rogers turned again to Susan.

'I understand that you were in the kitchen just now when your father was making tea for Lady Camilla Prendergast?' he said.

'That's right.' Susan looked genuinely puzzled, but her eyes were wary and defiant.

'He says that you helped him to make the tea. Is that so?'

'I filled the pot from the kettle, that's all.'

'*Was* that all?'

'Yes, of course it was. The kettle was boiling and Dad was cutting bread and butter and I said, "Shall I fill the pot?" and he said, "Yes", and I did.'

There was a long, uncomfortable pause, and then Susan added in a voice that had the edge of fear to it, 'There was nothing wrong with the tea, was there?'

'There was poison in it,' said Rogers briefly.

174

Her hand flew up to her mouth as though to suppress a scream.

'Poison?' she murmured. 'In the tea what Dad made?'

'In the tea you made together.'

'But I never did anything, I tell you, except put the boiling water in when Dad told me. What should I want to poison anyone for?'

'You knew that tea was for Lady Camilla, didn't you?'

'Has anything happened to her?' asked Susan swiftly.

'Nothing has happened to Lady Camilla. You know quite well that she did not drink the tea. Mrs Carstairs did.'

'What's happened to *her?*' The girl's face had become cold and sullen again.

'Mrs Carstairs is dead.'

'Well, that's not my fault, is it?' She displayed no more emotion now than if she had been unjustly rebuked for breaking a piece of china.

'What were you doing outside Lady Camilla's door?' asked Rogers suddenly.

'I went up there because I wanted to talk to her.'

'What should you want to talk to Lady Camilla about?'

'We'd had some words this morning when I went to sit in his lordship's room and I – well—'

'You wanted to have some more words with her, was that it?'

Susan shrugged her shoulders. 'It doesn't matter now,' she said. 'I didn't see her, anyway.'

'You went up there to see whether she had drunk the tea, didn't you?'

'I tell you, I didn't know anything about the tea,' Susan

repeated angrily. 'When I got there, there was Mrs Carstairs just coming out. She said her ladyship was asleep and not to be disturbed. We had some words, and then she took the tea away to her room and I went off to mine. That's all.'

'You made no attempt to stop Mrs Carstairs taking the tea which you knew was intended for Lady Camilla?'

'Why should I? I tell you I didn't know——'

'Very well, Mrs Warbeck. You needn't say it again. I don't think I need trouble you any further now. You understand that you may be asked questions about this later on, by other people?'

'They'll only get the same answers,' said Susan, and walked defiantly to the door.

When she had gone Dr Bottwink said, 'I apologise, Sergeant, for my outburst just now, but I was taken aback. This young person is the widow of the Honourable Mr Warbeck, I suppose?'

Rogers nodded.

'That is certainly a fact to be taken into consideration, along with the others. How long have you known this, may I ask?'

'Only since this afternoon.'

'So! And the others, they knew of it also?'

'Apart from Briggs, nobody knew it until today. Sir Julius learned of it only after Lord Warbeck's death.'

'And the ladies?'

'Only Lady Camilla was told. That was just before lunch.'

'I see.' The historian remained sunk in thought for a full minute before he spoke again, and then it was to himself, and with apparent irrelevance. 'The vocabulary of the uneducated classes is very limited,' he murmured. 'Unfortunately, it is also lacking in precision. Otherwise, there would be here a clue that might, perhaps, merit investigation. Yet, even so, I do not see that it will materially assist.'

'What were you saying?' asked Rogers.

'I? Nothing. I was, as I believe the expression is, speaking out of my turn. You have now all the facts you sought, Sergeant?'

'I think so.'

'So be it.' Dr Bottwink yawned prodigiously, and turned to stare into the fire.

There was the sound of heavy footsteps hurrying outside. The door burst open and Julius appeared. He was pink with excitement and his fatigue seemed for the time being to have vanished.

'Rogers!' he exclaimed. 'Rogers! Look at this, man!'

In his fat fist he held a small, dark object which he waved triumphantly to and fro.

'In my wardrobe!' he panted. 'In the drawer where I keep my handkerchiefs! I went to get myself a clean one just now, and when I took it away, there was this, lying just underneath!'

With the air of a card-player producing the ace of trumps, he set down on the library table a little blue glass bottle, prominently labelled 'Poison'.

'What d'you think of that?' asked Sir Julius.

XVII

'Words, words . . .'

Sergeant Rogers picked the bottle up and held it against the light.

'Empty, I see,' he said, and put it down again. His face was as expressionless as ever.

'Well?' said Julius, eagerly. 'Isn't that the thing you are looking for?'

'It seems so, Sir Julius. Briggs will be able to identify it, no doubt.' His tone was unenthusiastic, almost uninterested.

'And it was in my wardrobe, of all places! How the devil did it get there, do you suppose?'

'Well, sir, your room is readily accessible from the stairs. Once on the landing, it is the first door one comes to.'

'Quite. Next door to Lady Camilla's, in fact. Mrs Carstairs' room is just beyond.'

'I have that in mind, sir.'

'You searched their rooms last night, I suppose?'

'Yes, sir.'

'Then, how—?'

'I have no suggestions to offer, sir. And unless the person who put it there chooses to tell us, I see no means of finding out.'

The disapproval in the sergeant's voice was too plain to be ignored.

'I suppose,' faltered Sir Julius, 'I should have left it where it was until you could see it.'

'You should, sir.'

'There might have been fingerprints on it, and so on.'

'There *was* the possibility of fingerprints, certainly.'

'I am sorry. It was stupid of me. I'm afraid I rather lost my head when I saw it there.'

'I quite understand, sir.' Rogers paused before he went on, a little ominously, 'No doubt the officer who takes charge of this case in due course will accept your explanation, in view of your position.'

'Good God, Rogers, I should hope so!' Julius exploded.

'He will, of course, have to take account of the fact that there is no corroboration of your statement of how this was found.'

'Tchah!' said Sir Julius.

'However,' Rogers went on smoothly, 'there is one point as to which I shall be able to satisfy him. It was not in your wardrobe when I searched it last night. Let me see, you say it was underneath the top handkerchief in the pile just now?'

'Yes.'

'I opened that drawer when I was assisting you to change your clothes this afternoon. If anything had been disarranged there at the time, I think I should have observed it. I cannot be sure, but I think I should. That may help to limit further the period in which it was placed there.'

Rogers picked up the bottle and put it in his pocket.

'There is nothing else you would like to tell me about this, sir?' he asked.

'There is nothing else I can tell you. You have all the facts.'

'There is one fact,' observed Dr Bottwink, 'which is to me, at least, of some comfort.'

'What is that, sir?'

'The fact that this bottle is now empty. It means that I shall be able to eat my dinner with some degree of confidence.'

He got up and left the room. Whether for the reason he mentioned or not, he looked considerably less depressed than he had been. His face remained serious and thoughtful, but it had lost the look of blank dismay that it had worn ever since the tragedy of Mrs Carstairs had been discovered. He walked briskly enough to the north-east wing of the house, climbed the familiar, narrow stairs and found himself once more in the muniment room.

For once the haven failed to work its familiar spell. To all appearance it was unchanged. The roof had miraculously withstood the assaults of the weather. The archives still stood in their oak presses dry and intact. But now they cast their allurements in vain. Something had come between them and their impassioned suitor. The twentieth century, vulgar, discordant and disquieting, had invaded the stronghold of the eighteenth and put it to rout. To his own deep astonishment, Dr Bottwink found himself completely uninterested in the papers of the third Lord Warbeck.

He sat idle at his desk for several minutes before he confessed himself beaten. Then he laid down the pen with which he had been aimlessly playing and began to walk up and down the length of the narrow room. He had turned at the desk for the fourth time and was just approaching the door for the fifth when without warning it opened suddenly.

'Ah!' said Dr Bottwink, startled. 'Lady Camilla!'

'Am I disturbing you, Dr Bottwink?'

'That your ladyship should put me such a question! Disturbing me, indeed! When I consider my behaviour to you just now, believe me, I—'

'That's what I came to see you about,' said Camilla, cutting him short without ceremony. 'I rather think you owe me an explanation. Just what were you and all the others doing in my room?'

'It was an unhappy misunderstanding on my part. Perhaps, though,' he corrected himself pedantically, 'the adjective is inappropriate. I do not wish to give yet further offence. I am very happy in that I was mistaken. Quite simply, when I came into your room I thought you were dead.'

'You thought—! That is the oddest excuse I've ever heard for coming into a woman's room, and I've heard a good many.'

'It is true, none the less.'

'And why should I have been dead at that particular moment?'

'My lady,' said Dr Bottwink seriously, 'if I were to answer that question directly, I should perhaps be guilty of yet a further blunder. But may I remind you of what you yourself said this afternoon just before you went up to your room to rest yourself?'

Camilla shook her head.

'I don't remember,' she said.

'No? Let me repeat it. You said that this house smelled of death. You asked which of us would be the next to go.'

'Did I? I must have been in a pretty bad state to talk like that. It was very silly of me.'

Dr Bottwink stared at her in admiration.

'How wonderful are the recuperative powers of youth!' he said. 'A few hours of sleep and all is well again! But you did say that, Lady Camilla. And, you see, it turned out, unfortunately, that your words were not so silly, after all.'

'I don't quite understand.'

'You have not been told, then? Is it news to you that Mrs Carstairs is dead?'

'Mrs Carstairs!' Camilla blenched, but recovered herself admirably. 'What has happened?'

'She has been poisoned, my lady, apparently from the tea which was prepared for you and which she drank herself because she found you asleep.'

Camilla said nothing. She stood very rigid in the middle of the room, her fine eyes fixed upon Dr Bottwink's.

'I trust,' said the historian earnestly, 'that you were in truth asleep when Mrs Carstairs came to your room.'

'Did she come to my room? Certainly I was asleep if she did. I knew nothing about it.'

'That is well.' He sighed in relief. 'That is very well indeed. You will remember to tell the police that when they question you?'

'Of course.' Camilla looked more puzzled than ever. 'You understand, Dr Bottwink, don't you, that I haven't the least idea what you are talking about?'

'Be it so, my lady. Provided that you on your part will understand that in this matter I am your friend.'

'I think you are,' she said slowly. 'Though for the life of me I don't know why you should be.'

'For the life of me!' Dr Bottwink repeated. 'That is a slang expression, is it not? It is a suitable one, perhaps, for the situation we have been in. That reminds me, there is another phrase, Lady Camilla, which I have recently heard, on which I should be glad of your assistance. However proficient a foreigner may become in your language, I find there is still something to learn.'

'Really,' said Camilla, 'you are a very strange person! First you tell me that someone has tried to poison me and has poisoned Mrs Carstairs, and then you expect me to settle down to a quiet discussion about English slang! Are you – are you feeling all right, Dr Bottwink?'

'Thank you, my lady, I am perfectly sane. And I can assure you that I do not raise this matter out of idle curiosity, but because it may be of importance to both of us. Will you be good enough to bear with me and answer one single question?'

'Very well.'

'I am obliged.' Dr Bottwink adjusted his spectacles, put his hands behind his back, and raised his voice as though addressing a room full of students. 'My question is simply this. What meaning would you attach to the following phrase in the mouth of an individual of the working class: "I met So-and-so today; I had some words with him (or her)"?'

'Male or female individual?'

'Female.'

'In that case,' said Camilla without hesitation, 'I should say she said something pretty nasty to So-and-so.'

Dr Bottwink rubbed his hands.

'Excellent!' he said. 'And if the expression were: "We had some words"?'

'That would probably mean that the other woman answered back. It would be stronger, of course, if she said simply: "We had words." That would certainly mean a row.'

'That is a most delicate distinction. I have always maintained that English is the most expressive language in the world. Thank you very, very much.'

'Is that all, Dr Bottwink?'

The historian hesitated before he answered. 'Yes,' he said finally. 'There are some other questions I should like to put, but perhaps you would regard them as impertinent. Besides, there is somebody else whom I believe to be in a better position to answer them.'

'Oh! And who may that be?'

'Naturally, a female individual of the working class.'

The female individual of the working class was in the pantry with her father when Dr Bottwink found her. She looked at him with suspicion when he entered. Briggs was hardly more welcoming, but the correct formula came automatically to his lips.

'Were you requiring anything, sir?' he asked.

'Yes, Briggs. I should esteem it a great favour if with your permission I put an important question to Mrs Warbeck.'

'I'm not saying anything,' said Susan at once. 'I've told the sergeant everything that happened, and he says I shall have to say it again to the other police when they come. That's enough, isn't it?'

'May I assure you, madame, that the question is not one put to you already by the sergeant. I accept every word that you said to him.'

'I'm not saying anything,' she repeated.

'Briggs!' There were positively tears in Dr Bottwink's eyes as he turned towards the butler. 'Briggs, I implore your assistance! We are – all of us – under a shadow here. It rests with your daughter to deliver us. A simple statement that can in no way incriminate her – that she can deny to-morrow if she wishes – will you not help me to obtain it?'

'I think it is a matter for her to decide, sir,' said Briggs uncertainly. 'I'm sure I don't want to stand in your way, if you think it can help, but it's not my place to give orders, after what's happened. All the same, Susan, I don't see why you shouldn't do what the gentleman asks.'

'You're like all the rest!' Susan broke out. 'Badgering and bothering me about one thing and another! There's not a person in this house that hasn't been at me sooner or later, and now he has to start! Why can't they leave me alone?'

'Did Mrs Carstairs badger and bother you, madame?'

'She was the worst of the lot!'

'Ah!' Dr Bottwink breathed a sigh of relief. 'That was when you met her outside Lady Camilla's door, no doubt?'

Susan looked at him suspiciously.

'What do you know about that?' she asked.

'Nothing. You see, my child, we have arrived at the very question I wished to ask you. Tell me about Mrs Carstairs' badgering and bothering, and I think I can promise you that you will be neither badgered nor bothered again.'

'What's it got to do with you?'

'Perhaps nothing at all. Perhaps a great deal. I cannot tell until I hear. You and she had words, did you not?'

'It was all her fault if we did.'

'Naturally. I am not suggesting otherwise.'

'It was she began it.'

'Of course.'

'I shouldn't have said a word if she hadn't tried to come the high and mighty over me.'

'No doubt you were greatly provoked.'

'Well, you could hardly blame me speaking my mind, could you?'

'But certainly not!'

'I told her straight, "I'm not in your Sunday school, now," I said, "to be treated as a nobody. I expect to be spoken to respectful."'

'Indeed, yes. That was no more than just.'

'The impertinence of it! Her asking me what was I doing outside of her ladyship's door! I've a right to go where I like in this house, haven't I?'

'I should be the last to deny it of you, madame.'

'It gave her quite a turn, hearing me talk like that,' said Susan with reminiscent relish.

'It must have, indeed.'

'She said she wondered what the girls of today were coming to, and did I remember who I was speaking to. "I know who I'm speaking to all right," I told her, "I know that," I said. "That's not the question," I said. "Do you know who you're speaking to?" I asked her. "That's what I want to know."'

'Precisely.'

'"I'm the Honourable Mrs Warbeck," I said, "and what's

186

more, my little boy is the rightful Lord Warbeck now his grandfather's dead, as Sir Julius knows, and nobody's going to keep him out of his rights," I said, "nor me either."'

'My felicitations, madame. I was not aware of your good fortune. I trust his lordship is well. Is he with you now?'

'That's what she wanted to know, only she didn't put it like that. "Where is this brat?" she said. That's what she called his lordship – a brat! "Safe at home with his auntie," I said, "where nobody can get at him." And then she looked at me so fierce, if she hadn't had the tea-tray in her hands I believe she'd have gone for me.'

Dr Bottwink clicked his tongue in disapproval of such behaviour.

'The teacup was rattling in the saucer, she was that upset,' Susan went on. 'Trembling all over, she was. I thought next minute she'd drop the tray and all. And her face! Green, she was. Like she was going to be sick.'

'Yes, yes. Quite so.' Dr Bottwink nodded his head, his eyes half closed, as he tried to visualise the scene. 'Pray continue, madame.'

'Well, that's all that happened, really. She hadn't a word to say after that. I mean, how could she? She just turned away, leaving me standing where I was, and went down the passage to her own room. She was trying to walk haughty like, but she was still all of a tremble. When she gets to her own door she turns round and says, "I shall have tea in my own room," she says, "and please understand Lady Camilla is asleep and not to be disturbed." Still trying to be high and mighty, you see? But not succeeding, oh no! She was properly put down, I can tell you! Then she goes into her room and shuts the door, and that's the last I see of her.'

A long pause succeeded Susan's recital. The pantry seemed very quiet when her shrill voice was stilled at last. Briggs looked at his daughter in shocked silence. Dr Bottwink was silent too, but his face was serenely satisfied. When he finally spoke, it was in tones of profound relief.

'Thank you,' he said quietly. 'Thank you very much indeed. Mrs Warbeck, it is now only just that I should explain to you—'

Susan interrupted him.

'Dad,' she said to her father, 'isn't that a bell ringing somewhere?'

All three listened. A tinkling sound could be distinctly heard from the direction of the hall.

'God bless my soul, if it's not the telephone!' Briggs exclaimed. And forgetting the training of years, he ran to answer it, without even stopping to remove his apron or put on his coat.

XVIII

An English Murder

When Briggs, Dr Bottwink and Susan reached the hall, Sergeant Rogers was already in possession of the telephone. Julius was at his elbow. The three newcomers grouped themselves close behind him. A moment later, Camilla appeared on the staircase above and stood, leaning over the banister rail, watching the scene from above. Everybody was staring at the speaker and listening in a hushed silence, as though the spectacle of a man using the telephone was something so extraordinary that not a detail of it was to be missed. The conversation took some time, for the connection was imperfect, and Rogers had to repeat himself over and over again before he could make himself understood; but during it all, the little group remained motionless and intent. Only when it ended did they relax and become individuals again.

Hoarse and sweating, the sergeant put down the receiver and turned to face his audience.

'They will be here within a few hours, if all goes well,' he announced. 'At dawn tomorrow, at the latest. The road is clear as far as Warbeck village, and they are arranging for a ferry across the river. If there is no more rain, they should be able to take us out tomorrow.'

'Thank God!' murmured Julius. He was not normally a devout man, but he sounded as though he meant it.

Nobody else seemed to have anything to say at first. The prospect of release had apparently found them at a loss. They stood about irresolutely, shifting uneasily on their feet. Then Camilla from her post on the stairs made the obvious suggestion.

'Briggs,' she said, 'I think it would be a good idea if you brought us all drinks in the library.'

'Very good, my lady.' He turned to go and automatically beckoned Susan to accompany him.

'That includes your daughter, of course,' said Camilla in a clear, high voice. 'And bring some for yourself.'

'Yes, my lady.'

Briggs disappeared in haste. As he went, Camilla could see that the top of his bald head had flushed to a warm pink. She misinterpreted his emotion. It was inspired simply by the sudden realisation that he had allowed himself to appear before company in his shirtsleeves and apron.

Invested once more in his tail-coat, he returned a few minutes later to the library, bearing a tray laden with a decanter and glasses. He dispensed the drinks with grave ceremony, and then, taking his own glass, retired to a discreet distance near the door. With a fine sense of the appropriate, he had selected an old brown sherry of the type usually served at Warbeck Hall on the occasion of family funerals. The rest of the little assembly, grouped round the fire, sipped in silence. An air of anxious expectancy hung over the room.

It was Dr Bottwink who spoke first.

'So, Sergeant Rogers,' he said, in a loud voice that seemed to be addressed to the company at large, 'they will be here in a few hours' time, you say. The "they" you speak of are the police, I presume?'

'That is so, sir.'

'And when they come, what do you propose to tell them, may I ask?'

From his superior height, Rogers looked down on the squat figure with a weary air.

'I have already told you, sir,' he said patiently. 'I do not consider myself as being in charge of this case any longer. I shall simply place my report in their hands and leave the matter to them.'

'Your report – just so. It is in a state of completion, your report?'

Rogers emptied his glass and glanced at the clock.

'It is not altogether complete,' he said, 'but it will be very shortly. I have only a few additional facts to add so as to bring it up to date.'

Dr Bottwink also emptied his glass, but unlike Rogers he did not set it down. Instead he strolled over to the decanter and poured himself out another.

'I do not understand,' he observed, 'why these Markshire police – excellent fellows though they are, no doubt – should be in any better position than you in finding an answer to this problem.'

The sergeant shrugged his shoulders.

'That is not for me to say,' he said shortly, 'It doesn't happen to be my job, that's all.'

'I really think, Dr Bottwink,' put in Julius heavily, 'that it is hardly your place – the place of any of us, I may say – to dictate to the sergeant what he should or should not do. He knows his duty, and I am sure he requires no assistance in carrying it out.'

'As you please, Sir Julius. I am well aware of the

importance in this country of knowing one's place. And my place has certainly never been one in which I was in a position to dictate to anyone. Simply, it occurred to me that it might be of professional advantage to the sergeant if, when his colleagues arrived here, he was able not only to report the facts but to explain them. But if I have put myself forward improperly, I say no more.'

It took a little time for the significance of the stiff, pedantic sentences to sink into minds already dulled by emotion and fatigue. Camilla caught his meaning first.

'Dr Bottwink,' she said bluntly, 'do you know who killed Robert?'

'Of course.' He sipped his sherry and added, 'And Lord Warbeck. And Mrs Carstairs. It was all one and the same person.'

There was a sudden, sharp sound. Susan's sherry glass had slipped from her fingers and lay broken at her feet. Briggs came forward from his place by the door and impassively gathered up the fragments. Nobody else moved. Dr Bottwink did not so much as turn his head in the direction of the interruption. He was turning his own half-empty glass in his hand and looking down at it with a meditative smile. He showed no disposition to speak again.

'Go on, Dr Bottwink!' Camilla urged him. 'Go on!'

'What do you say, Sir Julius? Is it my place to speak? Or, rather,' he turned to Rogers, 'since this is essentially a police affair, perhaps you will advise me, Sergeant? Should I not, strictly speaking, reserve my confidences for the proper authorities when they get here?'

Sergeant Rogers had turned a bright red, and he spoke with difficulty.

'I understood you to say, sir,' he said, 'that you had already told me all that you knew. If you have any further information, you may reserve it until you make your statement to the officer who takes charge of this case. But you will have to explain to him why you thought fit to conceal it in the first place.'

'There is no question of concealment, Sergeant. I shall tell him just what I have told you. I shall tell him to read the life of William Pitt.' He glanced over towards one of the bookshelves and added, 'You have not, I perceive, taken my advice in the matter? You have not consulted that little work by the late Lord Rosebery?'

'No,' said Rogers, shortly. 'I have not.'

'A pity. But it is not too late. You have still time.'

'What is all this nonsense about William Pitt?' said Julius. 'I understood you to say that you had some theory about the death of my unfortunate relative who died last night. Now you run away from the point and start talking about someone who died a hundred years ago.'

'A good deal more than a hundred years ago. In 1806, to be precise. But that is a short time in the history of a country like England, where relics of the past are permitted not only to exist but to influence the present to a wholly lamentable degree.'

'If you think that, you know nothing whatever about modern England, sir!'

'Is that so? Then let me say that you know nothing about English history. Moreover, it is because of the indifference of you and your like to the lessons of your own past that your modern England is left riddled with antiquarian anachronisms. As an antiquarian myself, perhaps I should rejoice at such things, but when I find that the neglect of a simple reform, the necessity of which has been obvious and glaring since the year 1789 – if not earlier – has just now cost this country three lives, I think that as a nation you carry your conservatism too far!'

Quite plainly, Dr Bottwink felt that with his last re-sounding period he had completely crushed his adversary; and further, that, having crushed him, there was nothing more to be said. He turned his back on Sir Julius, replaced his glass on the tray, and was actually making for the door when Camilla intercepted him. She laid her hand on his arm and steered him back to the middle of the room, a look of patient determination on her face.

'Please don't be angry with us, Dr Bottwink,' she said. 'We aren't as clever as you, and we none of us know any history. We are all very tired and very frightened – at least, I know I am. Will you please, *please* put us out of our misery and explain what you have been talking about? You can start in 1789 if you really must, but do tell us something.'

Dr Bottwink was quite incapable of resisting such an appeal to his vanity.

'If you wish it, my lady,' he said, with a stiff little con-tinental bow. He took up a position in the exact centre of the carpet, his legs apart, his hands clasped behind his back, raised his chin and began in the clear, high tone of a lecturer:

'I have been invited to begin my exposition with the year 1789. In fact, I introduced the events of that year merely for the purpose of illustration or analogy. When, this morning, I invited Sergeant Rogers to consult the biography of the younger Pitt, I did so simply to bring to his attention a state of affairs which, it seemed to me, offered a ready-made explanation of the crime that he was investigating. I did not wish to push myself forward. I thought that by accepting my hint he would be able to solve the problem for himself. I thought that he would see – as I saw – that this case was a remarkable example of history repeating itself. I have to admit that subsequent events led me to doubt the validity of my own hypothesis. In the stress of the moment, I hastily assumed that my diagnosis was incorrect. Further enquiry, however, satisfied me that the error lay in this latter assumption and not in the original theory. In short, I had been perfectly right from the beginning. History *had* repeated itself – and to an even more remarkable degree than I had at first supposed.'

Dr Bottwink paused. He drew his handkerchief from his pocket, carefully polished his spectacles and readjusted them on his nose before proceeding: 'Sir Julius has characterised the events which we have recently witnessed as un-English. Respectfully, I beg to differ. This could only have happened in England. It is, indeed, an essentially English crime. I am a little astonished that he, of all persons, should have considered it otherwise. You may object,' the historian went on, though his audience, stunned by the flow of words, displayed not the slightest disposition to object, 'that crime – or at all events murder – is essentially a supra-national phenomenon; that consequently there can be no distinction between an English murder and an un-English one. But this is a fallacy. In investigating a crime we have to consider it in two aspects – the act itself, which is basically identical in all lands and under all systems of jurisprudence, and the social and political framework in which it occurs. To reduce the matter to the simplest possible terms, we must examine the motive for the crime. A motive that is valid for one form of society may be totally non-existent in another. And once the motive is determined, the identification of the criminal becomes a mere matter of simple deduction.'

Dr Bottwink removed his spectacles again. This time he folded them up and, retaining them in his hand, wagged them fiercely at his audience to drive home his points.

'Why, then, do I maintain that this was an English crime?' he demanded. 'Because the motive was English. Because it was made possible by a political factor that is peculiar to England.' He paused in momentary confusion. 'Perhaps I should have said "Britain",' he observed. 'Forgive me. I desire to offend nobody's susceptibilities. I am used to saying "England", and with your permission I shall continue to do so. To resume: this crime – and, for reasons which will become obvious, I use the singular and not the plural – this crime, then, could not have occurred but for the fact that England, alone of all civilised countries, retains in its constitution an hereditary legislative chamber. And its motive was quite simply to procure a seat in that chamber for one person by removing the two individuals who stood between him and the right to occupy it.'

'I have never heard such a pack of nonsense in my life!' Sir Julius, white with rage, advanced upon Dr Bottwink. Shaking his fist under the historian's nose, he spluttered, 'Do you dare to suggest, sir, that I—? Do you dare to suggest—?' The sentence trailed away into inarticulate sounds of anger.

Dr Bottwink remained literally and metaphorically un-moved. He did not budge an inch from his position, and he continued to speak without taking the smallest notice of the interruption.

'So far,' he proceeded in the same didactic manner, 'so far we have been considering what would appear at first sight to be a simple case of dynastic assassination. But the mat-ter is a little more complicated than that. If it were not so, I should have hardly been justified in characterising it as I have ventured to do. The destruction of a reigning family in the interests of a cadet branch is a practice common to all nations and all ages. In order to comprehend this inci-dent in its true light, it will be useful to revert once more to a consideration of the biography of William Pitt and the events of the year 1789.'

The lecture was at this point again interrupted, this time by Camilla. She had begun to take a cordial dislike to William Pitt, and at the renewed mention of his name she groaned aloud. But Dr Bottwink went remorselessly on.

'The year in question was one of many vicissitudes for this country and for Europe, but, interesting as they are in themselves, they are not relevant to this enquiry, for they were caused in the main by economic and constitutional factors here and abroad which are not now operative. As I ventured to point out to Sergeant Rogers this morning, its importance for our purposes lies precisely in an event *which did not happen.* Because it did not happen, it has been forgotten, except by historians, who unfortunately are not permitted to exercise much influence in current English politics. The event to which I allude – and which for some days appeared quite inevitable – was none other than the death, at that particular juncture, of the second Earl of Chatham. He had no son. His heir was none other than his brother, William Pitt, then Prime Minister and Chancellor of the Exchequer. One can but speculate on what would have ensued; but this much is certain: the great man's administration depended uniquely upon his personal ascendancy in what is still quaintly called the Lower House of Parliament. Had he been, in your own expressive phrase, kicked upstairs, the result would have been a major political crisis. Perhaps it is not too much to say that not only the career of a great statesman but the whole history of Europe turned upon the life or death of a totally undistinguished nobleman. Sir Julius,' he turned abruptly to the Chancellor of the Exchequer, still glowering at him within arm's length, 'does the parallel appeal to you?'

Sir Julius stared at the speaker in silence. His angry expression had been succeeded by one of unwilling admiration. Then, slowly and emphatically, he nodded his head.

'Your position is more vulnerable even than that of your illustrious predecessor, since constitutionally a Prime Minister may sit in the House of Lords. A Chancellor of the Exchequer, on the other hand, may not. Should it ever be your lot to succeed to the family peerage, you will be able to serve your country in any one of a variety of distinguished offices, but you will be for ever incapable of holding your present one. This fact must have been very much on your mind during the last twenty-four hours, must it not?'

Sir Julius nodded again.

'Why then,' the historian went on in an accent of gentle reproach, 'why did it never occur to you to reflect on who would be the obvious successor to that position when and if what Lord Rosebery has called "the grim humour of our constitution" compelled you to relinquish it? I am no student of contemporary politics, but I am sure that since I have been in this house I have heard the name mentioned a dozen times at least. Or was Mrs Carstairs wrong in her estimate of her husband's prospects?'

'She was perfectly right,' said Julius huskily. 'He is the obvious man.'

'Precisely.' Dr Bottwink threw out his hands in an expressive gesture. 'There is the case in a nutshell. Need I insult your intelligence by saying any more?'

'I think I owe you an apology,' said Julius, speaking with some difficulty.

'Not at all, Sir Julius. It was your innate modesty, no doubt, that clouded your vision, and prevented you from seeing that you were the person aimed at by the criminal all the time.'

It was a long time since Julius had been commended for this particular quality, and he flushed with pleasure.

'In conclusion,' Dr Bottwink went on, 'I think it will not be inappropriate if I express my sympathy with Sergeant Rogers. His primary function, as he has more than once emphasised, is to protect Sir Julius. He has performed it, no doubt, with assiduity and efficiency. But there was one danger against which he was powerless to protect his charge – the danger of an unwelcome elevation to the House of Lords. Sir Julius owes his escape from that, not to Scotland Yard, but to the happy circumstance that there existed, unknown to us all, an infant Lord Warbeck, upon whose birth I should like to tender to the Honourable Mrs

Warbeck my belated but sincere congratulations.'

The lecture was over. Dr Bottwink stepped down from an imaginary rostrum, put away his spectacles and became human once more. But at least one of his auditors was still unsatisfied.

'Dr Bottwink,' said Rogers. 'Do I understand you to suggest that Mrs Carstairs murdered Mr Robert Warbeck?'

'I deprecate the word "suggest", Sergeant. But I say she did.'

'And Lord Warbeck?'

'Certainly. That is to say, I have little doubt that it was she who broke to him the news of his son's death with the intention of hastening his own. It was hardly necessary for her purposes to precipitate the end of a dying man, but no doubt she was impatient.'

'Then will you tell me,' said Rogers heavily, 'who in your view killed Mrs Carstairs?'

'But I have answered that question already. Did I not say at the outset that one person was responsible for all three deaths? Mrs Carstairs, of course, killed herself.'

'I don't see any "of course" about it. Why should she do that?'

'But it is obvious, is it not? No, I have forgotten – you have not yet had the opportunity of investigating further the little episode that immediately preceded her suicide. I am referring to her interview with Mrs Warbeck outside the door of Lady Camilla's bedroom. Had you done so, as no doubt you would in the normal course, you would have learned that at that interview Mrs Warbeck informed her, in terms which were perhaps excusable in the circumstances but which I do not hesitate to describe as brusque, that the object for which she had just committed a daring crime had been wholly frustrated. Sir Julius was, after all, still a commoner, still standing between her husband and the post which she so ardently coveted for him. The heir to the honours of the house of Warbeck was beyond her reach. The reaction to this news was too much for a nervous system which must have been already strung nearly to breaking point. I need hardly elaborate what followed. The mechanics of the suicide are matters for you and your colleagues of the police. But I would suggest that the state of her shoes and the marks upon the carpet indicate that the poison was secreted in the snow, which until this afternoon was deep upon the balcony of her room. She recovered the bottle, emptied it into her tea, and then, as a final gesture of contempt – or perhaps – who knows? – in the hope of casting suspicion upon Sir Julius that would blast his career as effectively as would a peerage – deposited it in his wardrobe. That done, she returned to her room, poured out the tea and so performed the last act of despair.'

He stopped abruptly and silence fell upon the room. Then Briggs stepped forward from his corner and said something to Camilla in a low tone. She nodded and he left the room.

'Dinner will be ready in twenty minutes,' she said. 'It will only be cold scraps, so nobody need dress. Susan, you will dine with us, won't you? I want to hear all about Robert's boy.'

'So do I, by Jove!' exclaimed Sir Julius. 'He's a very important person now, as I hope you realise.'

'I know that, thank you,' said Susan pertly. 'It isn't every baby as is a lord at his age.'

'It isn't every baby,' he rejoined, 'that has the political career of a man like *me* dependent on him.'

'Would it not be an additional safeguard,' suggested Dr Bottwink, 'if the British constitution were rationalised to some degree? You have had a close squeak, like William Pitt before you. The next man may not be so lucky.'

'I shall speak to the Prime Minister about it,' said Sir Julius Warbeck.

also by Cyril Hare

ff

In *Untimely Death*, Francis Pettigrew travels to Exmoor for a holiday – an area in which as a young boy he was traumatised by coming across a dead body on the moor. In an attempt to exorcise this trauma, Pettigrew walks to the spot – only to find another dead body . . .

ff

In *Where the Wind Blows*, famous solo violinist Lucy Carless is making a guest appearance with the provincial Markshire Orchestra, only to be found strangled by a silk stocking partway through the concert. Everyone in the orchestra had access to the scene of the crime, and Inspector Trimble has no idea where to start. Luckily, retired barrister Francis Pettigrew is treasurer of the orchestra, and soon finds himself involved in the investigation.

ff

Tragedy at Law follows self-important High Court judge Mr Justice Barber as he moves from town to town presiding over cases. When an anonymous letter arrives for him, he dismisses it as the work of a harmless lunatic, but then events occur that make him fear for his life. Enter barrister and amateur detective Francis Pettigrew – can he find out who wants to kill Barber before it is too late?

'Elegant writing, wry humour, brilliant evocation of place, an intriguing mystery and a solution which draws on his personal experience of the law.' P. D. James